This was her one chance, the only time she had every right to put her lips on this man, and she wasn't missing the opportunity.

The other people in the room vanished as she reached out and flattened her palms on Jonas's lapels. He leaned in and put one hand on her jaw, guiding it upward. His warmth bled through her skin, enlivening it, and then her brain ceased to function as his mouth touched hers.

Instantly, that wasn't enough and she pressed forward, seeking more of him. The kiss deepened as his lips aligned properly and, oh, yes, that was it.

Her crush exploded into a million little pieces as she tasted what it was like for Jonas to kiss her. That nice, safe attraction she had been so sure she could hide gained a whole lot of teeth, slicing through her midsection with sharp heat. The dimensions of sensation opened around her, giving her a tantalizing glimpse of how truly spectacular it would feel if he didn't stop.

But he did stop, stepping back so quickly that Viv almost toppled over, but he caught her forearms and held her steady...though he looked none too steady himself, his gaze enigmatic and heated in a way she'd never witnessed before.

* * *

Best Friend Bride is part of the In Name Only trilogy:

"I do" should solve all their problems,
but love has other plans...

Dear Reader,

Interconnected stories are my favorite, especially when they're centered on the heroes. So when I started brainstorming for my next series, I got really excited as three best friends from college popped into my head. I couldn't wait to find out what they had in common, what bonded them together and why they'd be tough nuts to crack in the romance department. Boy, did my guys surprise me! It turns out they share a deep, dark aversion to love due to a tragedy the three endured their senior year. As adults, they continue to avoid relationships, but luckily, three special ladies arrive on the scene to help them understand that love is not so easily dismissed.

Best Friend Bride stars our first hero, Jonas Kim, who needs a temporary wife but not the hassle of a relationship he doesn't intend to prolong. Fortunately, he has a friend who fills the bill. Viviana Dawson is happy to do Jonas this favor for reasons of her own...namely that she has a huge secret crush on him! If he finds out, it's all over. But it's harder than either of them imagined to stay in the friend zone once they get behind closed doors. And how will the tragedy in Jonas's past affect their burgeoning romance? Hint: *a lot*!

I hope you enjoy the In Name Only series! The next two books are coming to you soon. Find me online at katcantrell.com.

Kat Cantrell

KAT CANTRELL

—

BEST FRIEND BRIDE

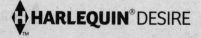

Recycling programs
for this product may
not exist in your area.

ISBN-13: 978-0-373-83858-5

Best Friend Bride

Copyright © 2017 by Kat Cantrell

Printed in U.S.A.

USA TODAY bestselling author **Kat Cantrell** read her first Harlequin novel in third grade and has been scribbling in notebooks since she learned to spell. She's a Harlequin So You Think You Can Write winner and a Romance Writers of America Golden Heart® Award finalist. Kat, her husband and their two boys live in north Texas.

Books by Kat Cantrell

Harlequin Desire

Marriage with Benefits
The Things She Says
The Baby Deal
Pregnant by Morning
The Princess and the Player
Triplets Under the Tree
The SEAL's Secret Heirs
An Heir for the Billionaire
The Marriage Contract

Happily Ever After, Inc.

Matched to a Billionaire
Matched to a Prince
Matched to Her Rival

Love and Lipstick

The CEO's Little Surprise
A Pregnancy Scandal
The Pregnancy Project
From Enemies to Expecting

In Name Only

Best Friend Bride

Visit her Author Profile page at Harlequin.com, or katcantrell.com, for more titles.

One

Jonas Kim would typically describe himself as humble, but even he was impressed with the plan he'd conceived to outwit the smartest man he knew— his grandfather. Instead of marrying Sun, the nice woman from a prominent Korean family, a bride Grandfather had picked out, Jonas had proposed to Viviana Dawson. She was nice, too, but also his friend and, more importantly, someone he could trust not to contest the annulment when it came time to file it.

Not only was Viv amazing for agreeing to this ridiculous idea, she made excellent cupcakes. It was a win all the way around. Though he could have done without the bachelor party. So not his thing.

At least no strippers had shown up. Yet.

He and his two best buddies had flown to Vegas this morning and though Jonas had never been to the city of sin before, he was pretty sure it wouldn't take much to have naked women draped all over the suite. He could think of little he'd like less. Except for marrying Sun. That he would hate, and not only because she'd been selected on his behalf. Sun was a disaster waiting to happen that would happen to someone else because Jonas was marrying Viv tomorrow in what would go down as the greatest favor one friend had ever done for another.

"Sure you wanna do this?" Warren asked as he popped open the bottle of champagne.

Also a bachelor party staple that Jonas could have done without, but his friends would just laugh and make jokes about how Jonas needed to loosen up, despite being well aware that he had been raised in an ultraconservative family. Grandfather had a lot of traditional ideas about how a CEO should act, and Jonas hadn't landed that job, not yet. Besides, there was nothing wrong with having a sense of propriety.

"Which part?" Jonas shot back. "The bachelor party or inviting you morons along?"

Hendrix, the other moron, grinned and took his glass of champagne from Warren. "You can't get married without a bachelor party. That would be sad."

"It's not a real wedding. Therefore, one would

assume that the traditions don't really have to be observed."

Warren shook his head. "It is a real wedding. You're going to marry this woman simply to get out of having a different bride. Hence my question. Are you sure this is the only way? I don't get why you can't just tell your grandfather thanks but no thanks. Don't let him push you around."

They'd literally been having the exact same argument for two weeks. Grandfather still held the reins of the Kim empire closely to his chest. In Korea. If Jonas had any hope of Grandfather passing those reins to him so he could move the entire operation to North Carolina, he had to watch his step. Marrying a Korean woman from a powerful family would only solidify Jonas's ties to a country that he did not consider his home.

"I respect my elders," Jonas reminded Warren mildly. "And I also respect that Sun's grandfather and my grandfather are lifelong friends. I can't expose her or it might disrupt everything."

Sun had been thrilled with the idea of marrying Jonas; she had a secret—and highly unsuitable— lover she didn't want anyone to find out about and she'd pounced on the idea of a husband to mask her affair. Meanwhile, their grandfathers were cackling over their proposed business merger once the two families were united in marriage.

Jonas wanted no part of any of that. Better to solve the problem on his own terms. If he was already married, no one could expect him to honor his grand-father's agreement. And once the merger had gone through, he and Viv could annul their marriage and go on with Jonas's integrity intact.

It was brilliant. Viv was the most awesome person on the planet for saving his butt from being burned in this deal. Tomorrow, they'd say some words, sign a piece of paper and poof. No more problems.

"Can you guys just be happy that you got a trip to Vegas out of this and shut up?" Jonas asked, and clinked glasses with the two men he'd bonded with freshman year at Duke University.

Jonas Kim, Hendrix Harris and Warren Garinger had become instant friends when they'd been as-signed to the same project group along with Marcus Powell. The four teenagers had raised a lot of hell together—most of which Jonas had watched from the sidelines—and propped each other up through everything the college experience could throw at them. Until Marcus had fallen head over heels for a cheerleader who didn't return his love. The aftermath of that still affected the surviving three members of their quartet to this day.

"Can't. You said no strippers," Hendrix grumbled, and downed his champagne in one practiced swal-low. "Really don't see the point of a bachelor party in Las Vegas if you're not going to take full advan-tage of what's readily available."

Jonas rolled his eyes. "Like you don't have a

wide array of women back in Raleigh who would get naked for you on demand."

"Yeah, but I've already seen them," he argued with a wink. "There are thousands of women whose breasts I've yet to ogle and I've been on my best behavior at home. What happens in Vegas doesn't affect my mom's campaign, right?"

Hendrix's mom was running for governor of North Carolina and had made him swear on a stack of Bibles that he would not do anything to jeopardize her chances. For Hendrix, that meant a complete overhaul of his social life, and he was feeling the pinch. So far, his uncanny ability to get photographed with scantily clad women hadn't surfaced, but he'd just begun his vow of chastity, so there was plenty of opportunity to cause a scandal if he really put his mind to it.

"Maybe we could focus on the matter at hand?" Warren suggested, and ran his fingers through his wavy brown hair as he plopped down on the love seat near the floor-to-ceiling glass wall of the Sky Suite they'd booked at the Aria. The dizzying lights of Vegas spread out in a panoramic view sixty stories below.

"Which is?"

Warren pointed his glass at Jonas. "You're getting married. Despite the pact."

The pact.

After the cheerleader had thoroughly eviscerated Marcus, he'd faded further and further away until eventually, he'd opted to end his pain permanently. In the aftermath of his death, the three friends had sworn to never let love destroy them as it had Marcus. The reminder sobered them all.

"Hey, man. The pact is sacred," Jonas said with a scowl. "But we never vowed to remain single the rest of our lives. Just that we'd never let a woman take us down like that. Love is the problem, not marriage."

Once a year, the three of them dropped whatever they were doing and spent the evening honoring the memory of their late friend. It was part homage, part reiteration of the pact. The profoundly painful incident had affected them in different ways, but no one would argue that Warren had taken his roommate's suicide harder than anyone save Marcus's mother.

That was the only reason Jonas gave him a pass for the insult. Jonas had followed the pact to the letter, which was easier than he'd ever let on. First of all, a promise meant something to him.

Second, Jonas never got near a woman he could envision falling in love with. That kind of loss of control…the concept made his skin crawl. Jonas had too much to lose to let a woman destroy everything he'd worked for.

Warren didn't look convinced. "Marriage is the gateway, my friend. You can't put a ring on a woman's finger and expect that she won't start dreaming of romantic garbage."

"Ah, but I can," Jonas corrected as he let Hendrix top off his champagne. "That's why this plan is so great. Viv knows the score. We talked about exactly what was going to happen. She's got her cupcake business and has no room for a boyfriend, let alone a permanent husband. I wouldn't have asked her to do this for me if she wasn't a good friend."

A friend who wasn't interested in taking things deeper. That was the key and the only reason Jonas had continued their friendship for so long. If there was even a possibility of getting emotional about her, he'd have axed their association immediately, just like he had with every other woman who posed a threat to the tight rein he held on his heart.

Hendrix drank straight from the champagne bottle to get the last few drops, his nearly colorless hazel eyes narrowed in contemplation as he set the empty bottle on the coffee table. "If she's such a good friend, how come we haven't met her?"

"Really? It's confusing to you why I'd want to keep her away from the man voted most likely to corrupt a nun four years in a row?"

With a grin, Hendrix jerked his head at Warren. "So Straight and Narrow over there should get the thumbs-up. Yet she's not allowed to meet him either?"

Jonas shrugged. "I'll introduce you at the ceremony tomorrow."

When it would be unavoidable. How was he supposed to explain that Viv was special to a couple of knuckleheads like his friends? From the first moment he'd met her, he'd been drawn to her sunny smile and generosity.

The little bakery near the Kim Building called Cupcaked had come highly recommended by Jonas's admin, so he'd stopped in to pick up a thank-you for his staff. As he'd stood in the surprisingly long line to place his order, a pretty brown-haired woman had exited from the back. She'd have captured his interest regardless, but when she'd stepped outside to slip a cupcake to a kid on the street who'd been standing nose pressed to her window for the better part of fifteen minutes, Jonas couldn't resist talking to her.

He'd been dropping in to get her amazing lemon cupcakes for almost a year now. Sometimes Viv let him take her for coffee to someplace where she didn't have to jump behind the counter on the fly, and occasionally she dropped by the Kim Building to take Jonas to lunch.

It was an easy, no-pressure friendship that he valued because there was no danger of him falling in too deep when she so clearly wasn't interested in more. They weren't sleeping together, and that kind of relationship wouldn't compute to his friends.

Didn't matter. He was happy with the status quo. Viv was doing him a favor and in return, he'd make it up to her with free business consulting advice for the rest of her life. After all, Jonas had singlehandedly launched Kim Electronics in the American market and had grown revenue to the tune of $4.7 billion last year. She could do worse than to have his undivided attention on her balance sheet whenever she asked, which he'd gladly make time for.

All he had to do was get her name on a marriage certificate and lie low until his grandfather's merger went through. Then Viv could go back to her single cupcake-baker status and Jonas could celebrate dodging the bullet.

Warren's point about marriage giving a girl ideas about love and romance was pure baloney. Jonas wasn't worried about sticking to the pact. Honor was his moral compass, as it was his grandfather's. Love represented a loss of control that other men might fall prey to, but not Jonas. He would never betray his friends or the memory of the one they'd lost.

All he had to do was marry a woman who had no romantic feelings for him.

Viviana Dawson had dreamed about her wedding day a bunch of times and not once had she imagined the swirl in her gut, which could only be described as a cocktail of nerves and *holy crap*.

Jonas was going to be her husband in a few short minutes and the anticipation of *what if* was killing her.

Jonas Kim had asked her to marry him. *Jonas*. The man who had kept Viv dateless for almost a year because who could measure up to perfection? Nobody.

Oh, sure, he'd framed it all as a favor and she'd accepted under the premise that they'd be filing for annulment ASAP. But still. She'd be Mrs. Kim for as long as it lasted.

Which might be short indeed if he figured out she had a huge crush on him.

He wasn't going to figure it out. Because *oh, my God.* If he did find out…

Well, he couldn't. It would ruin their friendship for one. And also? She had no business getting into a serious relationship, not until she figured out how to do and be whatever the opposite was of what she'd been doing and being with men thus far in her adult dating life.

Her sisters called it clingy. She called it committed. Men called it quits.

Jonas was the antidote to all that.

The cheesy chapel wasn't anything close to the venue of her fantasies, but she'd have married Jonas in a wastewater treatment plant if he'd asked her to. She pushed open the door, alone and not too happy about it. In retrospect, she should have insisted one of her sisters come to Vegas with her. Maybe to act as her maid of honor.

She could really use a hand to hold right about now, but no. She hadn't told any of her sisters she was getting married, not even Grace, who was closest to her in age and had always been her confidante. Well, until Grace had disappeared into her own family in much the same fashion as their other two sisters had done.

Viv was the cute pony in the Dawson family stable of Thoroughbreds. Which was the whole reason Viv hadn't mentioned her quickie Vegas wedding to a man who'd never so much as kissed her.

She squared her shoulders. A fake marriage was exactly what she wanted. Mostly.

Well, of course she wanted a real marriage eventually. But this one would get her into the secret club that the rest of the married Dawson sisters already belonged to. Plus, Jonas needed her. Total win across the board.

The chapel was hushed and far more sacrosanct than she'd have expected in what was essentially the drive-through lane of weddings. The quiet scuttled across her skin, turning it clammy. She was really doing this. It had all been conceptual before. Now it was real.

Could you have a nervous breakdown and recover in less than two minutes? She didn't want to miss a second of her wedding. But she might need to sit down first.

And then everything fell away as she saw Jonas in a slim-fitting dark suit that showcased his wiry frame. His energy swept out and engulfed her, as it always had from that first time she'd turned to see him standing outside her shop, his attention firmly on her instead of the sweet treats in the window.

Quick with a smile, quicker with a laugh, Jonas Kim's beautiful angular face had laced Viv's dreams many a night. He had a pretty rocking body, too. He kept in great shape playing racquetball with his friends, and she'd spent hours picturing him shirtless, his chest glistening as he swung a racket. In short, he was a truly gorgeous individual who she could never study long enough to sate herself.

Jonas's dark, expressive eyes lit up as he caught sight of her and he crossed the small vestibule to sweep her into a hug. Her arms came up around his waist automatically. How, she had no idea, when this was literally the first time he'd ever touched her.

He even smelled gorgeous.

And now would be a great time to unstick her tongue from the roof of her mouth. "Hey."

Wonderful. They'd had spirited debates on everything from the travesty of pairing red wine with fish to the merits of the beach over the mountains. Shakespeare, *The Simpsons*. But put her in the arms of the man she'd been salivating over for months and the power of speech deserted her.

He stepped back. Didn't help. And now she was cold.

"I'm so glad you're here," he said, his smooth voice ruffling all her nerve endings in the most delicious way. Despite being born in North Carolina, he had almost no accent. Good thing. He was already devastating enough.

"Can't have a wedding with no bride," she informed him. Oh, thank God, she could still talk, Captain Obvious moment aside. "Am I dressed okay for a fake marriage?"

His intense eyes honed in on her. "You look amazing. I love that you bought a new dress for this."

Yeah, that was why she passed up the idiots who hit on her with lame lines like "Give me your number and I'll frost your cupcakes for you." Jonas paid attention to her and actually noticed things like what she wore. She'd picked out this yellow dress because he'd mentioned once that he liked the color.

Which made it all the more strange that he'd never clued in that she had a huge thing for him. She was either better at hiding it than she'd had a right to hope for, or he knew and mercifully hadn't mentioned it.

Her pulse sped out of control. He didn't know, she repeated silently. Maybe a little desperately.

There was no way he could know. He'd never have asked her to do this marriage favor otherwise.

She'd been faking it this long. No reason to panic.

"I wanted to look good," she told him. *For you.* "For the pictures."

He smiled. "Mission accomplished. I want you to meet Warren."

Jonas turned, absently putting his arm around her and oh, that was nice. They were a unit already, and it had seemed to come so naturally. Did he feel it, too?

That's when she realized there was another man in the vestibule. Funny, she hadn't even noticed him, though she supposed women must fawn all over him, with those cheekbones and that expensive haircut. She held out her hand to the friend Jonas had talked endlessly about. "Nice to meet you. Jonas speaks very highly of you."

"Likewise," Warren said with a cryptic glance at Jonas. "And I'm sure whatever he's told you is embellished."

Doubtful when she didn't need Jonas's help to know that the energy drink company his friend ran did very well. You couldn't escape the logo for Flying Squirrel no matter where you looked.

Jonas waved that off with a smirk. "Whatever, man. Where's Hendrix?"

"Not my turn to babysit him." Warren shrugged, pulling out his phone. "I'll text him. He'll be here."

Somehow, Jonas seemed to have forgotten his arm was still around Viv's waist and she wasn't about to remind him. But then he guided her toward the open double doors that led to the interior of the chapel with firm fingers. Well, if this almost-intimacy was part of the wedding package, she'd take it.

"I'm not waiting on his sorry ass," Jonas called over his shoulder. "There are a thousand more couples in line behind us and I'm not losing my spot."

Warren nodded and waved, still buried in his phone.

"Some friends," Jonas murmured to her with a laugh, his head bent close. He was still taller than her even when she wore heels, but it had never been as apparent as it was today, since she was still tucked against his side as if he never meant to let go. "This is an important day in my life and you see how they are."

"I'm here." For as long as he needed her.

Especially if he planned to put his arm around her a whole bunch more. His warm palm on her waist had oddly settled her nerves. And put a whole different kind of butterfly south of her stomach.

Wow, was it hot in here or what? She resisted the urge to fan herself as the spark zipped around in places that *could not* be so affected by this man's touch.

His smile widened. "Yes, you are. Have I mentioned lately how much I appreciate that? The slot for very best friend in the whole world has just become yours, since clearly you're the only one who deserves it."

As reminders went, it was both brutal and necessary. This was a favor. Not an excuse for a man to get handsy with her.

Fine. Good. She and Jonas were friends, which was perfect. She had a habit of pouring entirely too much of herself into a man who didn't return her level of commitment. Mark had stuck it out slightly longer than Zachary, and she didn't like to think about how quickly she'd shed Gary and Judd. A sad commentary on her twenties that she'd had fewer boyfriends than fingers on one hand.

A favor marriage was the best kind because she knew exactly how it would end. It was like reading the last page of the book ahead of time, and for someone who loved surprise flowers but hated surprise discussions that started with "we have to talk," the whole thing sounded really great.

No pressure. No reason to get clingy and drive Jonas away with her neediness. She could be independent and witty and build her confidence with this marriage. It was a practice run with all the best benefits. He'd already asked her to move into his penthouse on Boylan Avenue. As long as she didn't mess up and let on how much she wanted to cling to every last inch of the man, it was all good.

Back on track, she smiled at the friend she was about to marry. They were friends with benefits that had nothing to do with sex. A point she definitely needed to keep in the forefront of her brain.

A lady in a puke-green suit approached them and verified they were the happy couple, then ran down the order of the ceremony. If this had been a real marriage, Viv might be a little disappointed in the lack of fanfare. In less than a minute, traditional organ music piped through the overhead speakers and the lady shoved a drooping bouquet at Viv. She clutched it to her chest, wondering if she'd get to keep it. One flower was enough. She'd press it into a book as a reminder of her wedding to a great man who treated her with nothing but kindness and respect.

Jonas walked her down the aisle, completely unruffled. Of course. Why would he be nervous? This was all his show and he'd always had a supreme amount of confidence no matter the situation.

His friend Warren stood next to an elderly man holding a Bible. Jonas halted where they'd been told to stand and glanced at her with a reassuring smile.

"Dearly beloved," the man began and was immediately interrupted by a commotion at the back. Viv and Jonas both turned to see green-suit lady grappling with the door as someone tried to get into the room.

"Sir, the ceremony has already started," she called out to no avail as the man who must be Hendrix Harris easily shoved his way inside and joined them at the front.

Yep. He looked just like the many, many pictures she'd seen of him strewn across the media, and not just because his mother was running for governor. Usually he had a gorgeous woman glued to his side and they were doing something overly sensual, like kissing as if no one was watching.

"Sorry," he muttered to Jonas. His eyes were bloodshot and he looked like he'd slept in his expensively tailored shirt and pants.

"Figured you'd find a way to make my wedding memorable," Jonas said without malice, because that's the kind of man he was. She'd have a hard time being so generous with someone who couldn't be bothered to show up on time.

The officiant started over, and in a few minutes, she and Jonas exchanged vows. All fake, she chanted to herself as she promised to love and cherish.

"You may kiss the bride," the officiant said with

so little inflection that it took a minute for it to sink in that he meant *Jonas* could kiss *her*. Her pulse hit the roof.

Somehow, they hadn't established what would happen here. She glanced at Jonas and raised a brow. Jonas hesitated.

"This is the part where you kiss her, idiot," Hendrix muttered with a salacious grin.

This was her one chance, the only time she had every right to put her lips on this man, and she wasn't missing the opportunity. The other people in the room vanished as she flattened her palms on Jonas's lapels. He leaned in and put one hand on her jaw, guiding it upward. His warmth bled through her skin, enlivening it, and then her brain ceased to function as his mouth touched hers.

Instantly, that wasn't enough and she pressed forward, seeking more of him. The kiss deepened as his lips aligned properly and oh, yes, that was it.

Her crush exploded into a million little pieces as she tasted what it was like to kiss Jonas. That nice, safe attraction she had been so sure she could hide gained teeth, slicing through her midsection with sharp heat. The dimensions of sensation opened around her, giving her a tantalizing glimpse of how truly spectacular it would feel if he didn't stop.

But he did stop, stepping back so quickly that she almost toppled over. He caught her forearms and held her steady…though he looked none too steady himself, his gaze enigmatic and heated in a way she'd never witnessed before.

Clearly that experience had knocked them both for a loop. What did you say to someone you'd just kissed and who you wanted to kiss again, but really, that hadn't been part of the deal?

"That was nice," Jonas murmured. "Thanks."

Nice was not the word on her mind. So they were going to pretend that hadn't just happened, apparently.

Good. That was exactly what they should do. Treat it like a part of the ceremony and move on.

Except her lips still tingled, and how in the world was Jonas just standing there holding her hand like nothing momentous had occurred? She needed to learn the answer to that, stat. Especially if they were going to be under the same roof. Otherwise, their friendship—and this marriage—would be toast the second he clued in to how hot and bothered he got her. He'd specifically told her that he could trust her because they were *friends* and he needed her to be one.

"I now pronounce you husband and wife," the officiant intoned, completely oblivious to how the earth had just swelled beneath Viv's feet.

Jonas turned and led her back up the aisle, where they signed the marriage license. They ended up in the same vestibule they'd been in minutes before, but now they were married.

Her signature underneath Jonas's neat script made

it official, but as she'd expected, it was just a piece of paper. The kiss, on the other hand? That had shaken her to the core.

How was she going to stop herself from angling for another one?

"Well," Hendrix said brightly. "I'd say this calls for a drink. I'll buy."

Two

Jonas had never thought of his six-thousand-square-foot penthouse condo as small. Until today. It was full of Viviana Dawson. Er, *Kim*. Viviana Kim. She'd officially changed her name at the Department of Motor Vehicles, and soon, she'd have a new driver's license that said she had the legal right to call herself that. By design. His sense of honor wouldn't permit him to outright lie about his relationship with Viv; therefore, she was Mrs. Kim in every sense of the word.

Except one.

The concept was surreal. As surreal as the idea that she was his wife and he could introduce her as such to anyone who asked.

Except for himself apparently because he was having a hard time thinking of her that way no matter how many times he repeated the word *wife* when he glimpsed her through the archway leading to the kitchen. Boxes upon boxes covered every inch of the granite countertops, and though she'd been working on unpacking them for an hour, it looked like she'd barely made a dent.

He should quit skulking around and get in there to help. But he hadn't because he couldn't figure out how to manage the weird vibe that had sprung up between them.

That *kiss*.

It had opened up a Pandora's box that he didn't know how to close. Before, he'd had a sort of objective understanding that Viv was a beautiful woman whose company he enjoyed.

Ever since the ceremony, no more. There was a thin veil of awareness that he couldn't shake. But he needed to. They were living together as *friends* because she'd agreed to a favor that didn't include backing her up against the counter so he could explore her lush mouth.

He liked Viv. Add a previously undiscovered attraction and she was exactly the kind of woman he'd studiously avoided for nearly a decade. The kind he could easily envision taking him deeper and deeper until he was emotionally overwhelmed enough to give up everything.

The problem of course being that he couldn't stop

calling her, like he usually did with women who threatened his vow. He'd married this one.

He was being ridiculous. What was he, seventeen? He could handle a little spark between friends, right? Best way to manage that was to ignore it. And definitely not let on that he'd felt something other than friendly ever since kissing her.

All he and Viv had to do was live together until he could convince his grandfather to go through with the merger anyway. Once the two companies signed agreements, neither would back out and Jonas was home free. Since he was covering Viv's rent until then, she could move back into her apartment at that point.

This plan would work, and soon enough, he could look back on it smugly and pinpoint the exact moment when he'd outsmarted his grandfather.

Casually, he leaned on the exposed-brick column between the dining room and the kitchen and crossed his arms like everything was cool between them. It *would* be cool. "What can I do?"

Viv jerked and spun around to face him, eyes wide. "You scared me. Obviously."

Her nervous laugh ruffled his spine. So they were both feeling the weirdness, but it was clearly different weirdness on her side than on his. She was jumpy and nervous, not hot and bothered. He had not seen that coming. That was…not good. "Sorry. I didn't mean to. We've both been living alone for so long that I guess we have to get through an adjustment period."

Which was the opposite of what he'd expected. They'd always been so relaxed with each other. How could they get back to that?

She nodded. "Yes, that's what I've been telling myself."

Was it that bad? Her forlorn voice tripped something inside him and it was not okay that she was uncomfortable around him now. "Best way to adjust is to spend time together. Let me help you put away these…" He grabbed a square glass dish from the counter. "Pans?"

"Pyrex." She smiled and it seemed like it came easier. "I can't imagine you care anything about where I put my bakeware."

He waggled his brows. "That depends on whether that's something you use to make cupcakes or not."

Her cupcakes weren't like the store-bought ones in the hard plastic clamshells. Those tasted like sugared flour with oily frosting. Viv's lemon cupcakes—a flavor he'd never have said he'd like—had a clean, bright taste like she'd captured lemonade in cake form.

"It's not. Casseroles."

"Not a fan of those." He made a face before he thought better of it.

Maybe she loved casseroles and he was insulting her taste. And her cooking skills. But he'd never said one word about her whipping up dinner for him each night, nor did he expect her to. She knew that. Right?

They had so much to learn about each other, especially if they were going to make this marriage seem as real as possible to everyone, except select few people they could trust, like Warren and Hendrix. If word got back to his grandfather that something wasn't kosher, the charade would be over.

And he'd invested way too much in this marriage to let it fail now.

His phone beeped from his pocket, and since the CEO never slept, he handed over the glass dish to check the message.

Grandfather. At 6:00 a.m. Seoul time. Jonas tapped the message. All the blood drained from his head.

"Jonas, what's wrong?" Viv's palm came to rest on his forearm and he appreciated the small bit of comfort even as it stirred things it shouldn't.

"My grandfather. My dad told him that we got married." Because Jonas had asked him to. The whole point had been to circumvent his grandfather's arranged-marriage plan. But this—

"Oh, no. He's upset, isn't he?" Viv worried her lip with her teeth, distracting him for a moment.

"On the contrary," Jonas spit out hoarsely. "He's thrilled. He's so excited to meet you, he got on a plane last night. He's here. In Raleigh. Best part? He talked my dad into having a house party to welcome you into the family. This weekend."

It was a totally unforeseen move. Wily. He didn't believe for a second that his grandfather was thrilled with Jonas's quick marriage or that the CEO of one of the largest conglomerates in Korea had willingly walked away from his board meetings to fly seven thousand miles to meet his new granddaughter-in-law.

This was something else. A test. An "I'll believe it when I see it." Maybe Grandfather scented a whiff of the truth and all it would take was one slipup before he'd pounce. If pressed, Jonas would feel honor bound to be truthful about Viv's role. The marriage could be history before dark.

A healthy amount of caution leaped into Viv's expression. "This weekend? As in we have two days to figure out how to act like a married couple?"

"Now you're starting to see why my face looks like this." He swirled an index finger near his nose, unbelievably grateful that she had instantly realized the problem. "Viv, I'm sorry. I had no idea he was going to do this."

The logistics alone… How could he tell his mom to give them separate bedrooms when they were essentially still supposed to be in the honeymoon phase? He couldn't. It was ludicrous to even think in that direction when what he should be doing was making a list of all the ways this whole plan was about to fall apart. So he could mitigate each and every one.

"Hey."

Jonas glanced up as Viv laced her fingers with his as if she'd done it many times, when in fact she hadn't. She shouldn't. He liked it too much.

"I'm here," she said, an echo of her sentiment at the wedding ceremony. "I'm not going anywhere. My comment wasn't supposed to be taken as a 'holy cow how are we going to do this.' It was an 'oh, so we've got two days to figure this out.' We will."

There was literally no way to express how crappy that made him feel. Viv was such a trouper, diving into this marriage without any thought to herself and her own sense of comfort and propriety. He already owed her so much. He couldn't ask her to fake intimacy on top of everything else.

Neither did he like the instant heat that crowded into his belly at the thought of potential intimate details. *He* couldn't fake intimacy either. It would feel too much like lying.

The only way he could fathom acting like he and Viv were lovers would be if they were.

"You don't know my grandfather. He's probably already suspicious. This house party is intended to sniff out the truth."

"So?" She shrugged that off far too easily. "Let him sniff. What's he going to find out, that we're really legally married?"

"That the marriage is in name only."

To drive the point home, he reached out to cup Viv's jaw and brought her head up until her gaze clashed with his, her mouth mere centimeters away from his in an almost-kiss that would be a real one with the slightest movement. She nearly jumped out of her skin and stumbled back a good foot until she hit the counter. And then she tried to keep going, eyes wide with…something.

"See?" he said. "I can't even touch you without all sorts of alarms going off. How are we going to survive a whole weekend?"

"Sorry. I wasn't—" She swallowed. "I wasn't expecting you to do that. So clearly the answer is that we need to practice."

"Practice what?" And then her meaning sank in. "Touching?"

"Kissing, too." Her chest rose and fell unevenly as if she couldn't quite catch her breath. "You said we would best get through the adjustment period by spending time together. Maybe we should do that the old-fashioned way. Take me on a date, Jonas."

Speechless, he stared at her, looking for the punch line, but her warm brown eyes held nothing but sincerity. The idea unwound in his gut with a long, liquid pull of anticipation that he didn't need any help interpreting.

A date with his wife. No, with Viv. And the whole goal would be to get her comfortable with his hands on her, to kiss her at random intervals until it was so natural, neither of them thought anything of it.

Crazy. And brilliant. Not to mention impossible.

"Will you wear a new dress?" That should not have been the next thing out of his mouth. *No* would be more advisable when he'd already identified a great big zone of danger surrounding his wife. But *yes* was the only answer if he wanted to pull off this plan.

She nodded, a smile stealing over her face. "The only caveat is no work. For either of us. Which means I get dessert that's not cupcakes."

Oddly, a date with Viv where kissing was expected felt like enough of a reward that he didn't mind that addendum so much, though giving up cupcakes seemed like a pretty big sacrifice. But as her brown eyes seared him thoroughly, the real sacrifice was going to be his sanity. Because he could get her comfortable with his hands on her, but there was no way to get *him* there.

The date would be nothing but torture—and an opportunity to practice making sure no one else realized that, an opportunity he could not pass up. Having an overdeveloped sense of ethics was very inconvenient sometimes.

"It's a deal. Pick you up at eight?"

That made her laugh for some reason. "My bedroom is next door to yours, silly. Are we going to have a secret knock?"

"Maybe." The vibe between them had loosened gradually to where they were almost back to normal, at least as far as she was concerned. Strange that the concept of taking Viv on a date should be the thing to do it. "What should it be?"

Rapping out a short-short-pause-short pattern,

she raised her brows. "That means we're leaving in five minutes so get your butt in gear."

"And then that's my cue to hang out in the living room with a sporting event on TV because you're going to take an extra twenty?"

Tossing her head, she grinned. "You catch on fast. Now, I have to go get ready, which means you get to unload the rest of these boxes."

Though he groaned good-naturedly as she scampered out of the kitchen, he didn't mind taking over the chore. Actually, she should be sitting on the couch with a drink and a book while he slaved for hours to get the house exactly the way she liked it. He would have, too, simply because he owed her for this, but she'd insisted that she wanted to do it in order to learn where everything was. Looked like a date was enough to trump that concept.

As the faint sound of running water drifted through the walls, he found spots in his cavernous kitchen for the various pieces Viv had brought with her to this new, temporary life. Unpacking her boxes ended up being a more intimate task than he'd anticipated. She had an odd collection of things. He couldn't fathom the purpose of many of them, but they told him fascinating things about the woman he'd married. She made cupcakes for her business but she didn't have so much as one cupcake pan in her personal stash. Not only that, each item had a well-used sheen, random scrapes, dents, bent handles.

Either she'd spent hours in her kitchen trying to

figure out what she liked to bake the most or she'd cleaned out an estate sale in one fell swoop. He couldn't wait to find out, because what better topic to broach on a date with a woman he needed to know inside and out before Friday night?

As he worked, he couldn't help but think of Viv on the other side of the walls, taking a shower. The ensuing images that slammed through his mind were not conducive to the task at hand and it got a little hard to breathe. He should not be picturing her "getting ready" when, in all honesty, he had no idea what that entailed. Odds were good she didn't lather herself up and spend extra time stroking the foam over her body like his brain seemed bent on imagining.

What was his *problem*? He never sat around and fantasized about a woman. He'd never felt strongly enough about one to do so. When was the last time he'd even gone on a date? He might stick Warren with the workaholic label but that could easily be turned back on Jonas. Running the entire American arm of a global company wasn't for wimps, and he had something to prove on top of that. Didn't leave a lot of room for dating, especially when the pact was first and foremost in his mind.

Of course the women he dated always made noises about not looking for anything serious and keeping their options open. And Jonas was always completely honest, but it didn't seem to matter if he flat-out said he wasn't ever going to fall in love. Mostly they took it as a challenge, and things got sticky fast, especially when said woman figured out he wasn't kidding.

Jonas was a champion at untangling himself before things went too far. Before *he* went too far. There were always warning signs that he was starting to like a woman too much. That's when he bailed.

So he had a lot of one-night stands that he'd never intended to be such. It made for stretches of lonely nights, which was perhaps the best side benefit of marriage. He didn't hate the idea of having someone to watch a movie with on a random Tuesday night, or drinking coffee with Viv in the morning before work. He hoped she liked that part of their marriage, too.

Especially since that was all they could ever have between them. It would be devastating to lose her friendship, which would surely happen if they took things to the next level. Once she found out about the pact, either she'd view it as a challenge or she'd immediately shut down. The latter was more likely. He'd hate either one.

At seven forty he stacked the empty boxes near the door so he could take them to the recycling center in the basement of the building later, then went to his room to change clothes for his date.

He rapped on Viv's door with the prescribed knock, grinning as he pictured her on the other side deliberately waiting for as long as she could to answer because they'd made a joke out of this new ritual. But she didn't follow the script and opened the door almost immediately.

Everything fled his mind but her as she filled the doorway, her fresh beauty heightened by the colors of her dress. She'd arranged her hair up on her head, leaving her neck bare. It was such a different look that he couldn't stop drinking her in, frozen by the small smile playing around her mouth.

"I didn't see much point in making you wait when I'm already ready," she commented. "Is it okay to tell you I'm a little nervous?"

He nodded, shocked his muscles still worked. "Yes. It's okay to tell me that. Not okay to be that way."

"I can't help it. I haven't been on a date in…" She bit her lip. "Well, it's been a little while. The shop is my life."

For some reason, that pleased him enormously. Though he shouldn't be so happy that they were cut from the same workaholic cloth. "For me, too. We'll be nervous together."

But then he already knew she had a lack in her social life since she'd readily agreed to this sham marriage, telling him she was too busy to date. Maybe together, they could find ways to work less. To put finer pleasures first, just for the interim while they were living together. That could definitely be one of the benefits of their friendship.

She rolled her eyes. "You're not nervous. But you're sweet to say so."

Maybe not nervous. But something.

His palms itched and he knew good and well

the only way to cure that was to put them on her bare arms so he could test out the feel of her skin. It looked soft.

Wasn't the point of the date to touch her? He had every reason to do exactly that. The urge to reach out grew bigger and rawer with each passing second.

"Maybe we could start the date right now?" she suggested, and all at once, the hallway outside her room got very small as she stepped closer, engulfing him in lavender that could only be her soap.

His body reacted accordingly, treating him to some more made-up images of her in the shower, and now that he had a scent to associate with it, the spike through his gut was that much more powerful. And that much more of a huge warning sign that things were spiraling out of control. He just couldn't see a good way to stop.

"Yeah?" he murmured, his throat raw with unfulfilled need. "Which part?"

There was no mistaking what she had in mind when she reached out to graze her fingertips across his cheek. Nerve endings fired under her touch and he leaned into her palm, craving more of her.

"The only part that matters," she whispered back. "The part where you don't even think twice about getting close to me. Where it's no big thing if you put your arm around my waist or steal a kiss as I walk by."

If that was the goal, he was failing miserably because it was a big thing. A huge thing. And getting bigger as she leaned in, apparently oblivious to the way her lithe body brushed against his. His control snapped.

Before he came up with reasons why he shouldn't, he pulled her into his arms. Her mouth rose to meet his and, when it did, dropped them both into a long kiss. More than a kiss. An exploration.

With no witnesses this time, he had free rein to delve far deeper into the wonders of his wife than he had at the wedding ceremony.

Her enthusiastic response was killing him. *His* response was even worse. How had they been friends for so long without ever crossing this line? Well, he knew how—because if they had, he would have run in the other direction.

He groaned as her fingers threaded through his hair, sensitizing everything she touched. Then she iced that cake with a tentative push of her tongue that nearly put him on his knees. So unexpected and so very hot. Eagerly, he matched her sweet thrust with his own. Deeper and deeper they spiraled until he couldn't have said which way was up. Who was doing the giving and who was greedily lapping it up.

He wanted more and took it, easing her head back with firm fingers until he found the right angle to get more of her against his tongue. And now he wanted more of her against his body.

He slid a hand down the curve of her spine until he hit a spot that his palm fit into and pressed until her hips nestled against his erection. Amazing. Perfect.

The opposite of friendly.

That was enough to get his brain in gear again. This was not how it should be between them, with all this raw need that he couldn't control.

He ended the kiss through some force of will he'd never understand and pulled back, but she tried to follow, nearly knocking herself off balance. Like she had at the ceremony. And in a similar fashion, he gripped her arms to keep her off the floor. It was dizzying how caught up she seemed to get. A rush he could get used to and shouldn't.

"Sorry," he said gruffly. "I got a little carried away."

"That's what was supposed to happen," she informed him breathlessly, "if we have any hope of your grandfather believing that we're deliriously happy together."

Yeah, that wasn't the problem he was most worried about at this moment. Viv's kiss-swollen lips were the color of raspberries and twice as tempting. All for show. He'd gotten caught up in the playacting far too easily, which wasn't fair to her. Or to his Viv-starved body that had suddenly found something it liked better than her cupcakes.

"I don't think anyone would question whether we spark, Viv," he muttered.

The real issue was that he needed to kill that spark and was pretty certain that would be impossible now.

Especially given the way she was gazing up at him with something a whole lot hotter than warmth in her brown eyes. She'd liked kissing him as much as he'd liked it. She might even be on board with taking things a step further. But they couldn't consummate this marriage or he could forget the annulment. Neither did he want to lead her on, which left him between a rock and an extremely hard place that felt like it would never be anything but hard for the rest of his life.

"In fact," he continued, "we should really keep things platonic behind closed doors. That's better for our friendship, don't you think?"

He'd kissed his wife and put his hands on her body because she'd told him to. And he was very much afraid he'd do it again whether it was for show or not unless he had some boundaries. Walking away from Viv wasn't an option. He had to do something that guaranteed he never got so sucked into a woman that she had power over his emotional center.

Thankfully, she nodded. "Whatever works best for you, Jonas. This is your fake marriage."

And how messed up was it that he was more than a little disappointed she'd agreed so readily?

Three

Viv hummed as she pulled the twenty-four-count pan from the oven and stuck the next batch of Confetti Surprise in its place. Customers thronged the showroom beyond the swinging door, but she kept an eye on things via the closed-circuit camera she'd had installed when she first started turning a profit.

Couldn't be too careful and besides, it made her happy to watch Camilla and Josie interact with the cupcake buyers while Viv did the dirty work in the back. She'd gotten so lucky to find the two college-aged girls who worked for her part-time. Both of them were eager students, and soon Viv would teach them the back-office stuff like bookkeeping and ordering. For now, it was great to have them running the register so Viv could focus on product.

Not that she was doing much focusing. Her mind wandered constantly to the man who'd kissed her so passionately last night.

Jonas had been so into the moment, so into her, and it had been heady indeed. Score one for Viv to have landed in his arms due to her casual suggestion that they needed to "practice." Hopefully he'd never clue in that she jumped when he touched her because he zapped a shock of heat and awareness straight to her core every dang time, no matter how much she tried to control it.

Of course, he'd shut it all down, rightfully so. They were friends. If he'd been interested in more, he would have made a move long before now.

Didn't stop her from wishing for a repeat.

A stone settled into her stomach as three dressed-to-the-nines women breezed through the door of her shop. On the monitor, she watched her sisters approach the counter and speak to Josie, oblivious to the line of customers they'd just cut in front of. Likely they were cheerfully requesting to speak with Viv despite being told countless times that this wasn't a hobby. She ran a business, which meant she didn't have time to dash off with them for tea, something the three housewives she shared parentage with but little else didn't seem to fully grasp.

Except she couldn't avoid the conversation they were almost certainly here for. She'd finally broken down and called her mother to admit she'd gotten married without inviting anyone to the wedding. Of course that news had taken all of five minutes to blast its way to her sisters' ears.

Dusting off her hands, Viv set a timer on her phone and dropped it into her pocket. Those cupcakes in the oven would provide a handy out if things got a little intense, and knowing Hope, Joy and Grace, that was likely. She pushed open the swinging door and pasted a smile on her face.

"My favorite ladies," she called with a wave and crossed the room to hug first Grace, her next-oldest sister, then Joy and Hope last. More than a few heads turned to check out the additions to the showroom. Individually, they were beautiful women, but as a group, her sisters were impressive indeed, with style and elegance galore.

Viv had been a late-life accident, but her parents tried hard not to make her feel like one. Though it was obvious they'd expected to have three children when they couldn't come up with a fourth virtue to name their youngest daughter. She'd spent her childhood trying to fit in to her own family and nothing had changed.

Until today. Finally, Viviana Kim had a new last name and a husband. Thanks to Jonas and his fake marriage deal, she was part of the club that had excluded her thus far. Just one of many reasons she'd agreed.

"Mom told us," Hope murmured, her social polish

in full force. She was nothing if not always mind-ful of propriety, and Viv appreciated it for once, as the roomful of customers didn't need to hear about Viv's love life. "She's hurt that you ran off to Vegas without telling anyone."

"Are you happy?" Grace butted in. She'd gotten married to the love of her life less than a year ago and saw hearts and flowers everywhere. "That's the important thing."

"Mom said you married Jonas Kim," Joy threw in before Viv could answer, not that she'd intended to interrupt before everyone had their say. That was a rookie mistake she'd learned to avoid years ago. "Surely his family would have been willing to make a discreet contribution to the ceremony. You could have had the wedding of the year."

Which was the real crime in Joy's mind—why spend *less* money when you could spend more, par-ticularly when it belonged to someone else? Joy's own wedding had garnered a photo spread in *Bride* magazine five years ago, a feat no other Raleigh bride had scored since.

It had been a beautiful wedding and Joy had been a gorgeous bride. Of course, because she'd been so happy. All three of her sisters were married to hand-some, successful men who treated them like royalty, which was great if you could find that. Viv had made do with what had been offered to her, but they didn't have to know that. In fact, she'd do everything in her power not to tip off her sisters that her marriage was anything but amazing. Was it so wrong to want them to believe she'd ended up exactly where she'd yearned to be for so long?

"Also, he's Korean," Hope added as if this might be news to Viv. "Mom is very concerned about how you'll handle the cultural differences. Have you discussed this with him?"

That was crossing a line. For several reasons. And Viv had had enough. "Jonas is American. He was born in the same hospital as you, so I'm pretty sure the cultural differences are minimal. Can you just be happy for me and stop with the third degree?"

All three women stared at her agape, even Grace, and Viv was ashamed at how good the speech had made her feel. She rarely stood up to the steam-roller of her sisters, mostly because she really did love them. But she was married now, just like they were, and her choices deserved respect.

"Jonas does make me happy," she continued, shooting Grace a smile. "But there's nothing to be concerned about. We've known each other for about a year and our relationship recently grew closer. That's all there is to it."

Despite the fact that it was absolute truth, prickles swept across her cheeks at the memory of how *close* they'd gotten last night.

An unconvinced expression stole over Hope's face. As the oldest, she took her role as the protector seriously. "We still don't understand why the secrecy. None of us even remember you so much as mentioning his name before."

"Of course we know who he *is*," Joy clarified. "Everyone in Raleigh appreciates that he's brought a global company to this area. But we had no idea you'd caught his eye."

Viv could read between those lines easily enough. She didn't wear nine-thousand-dollar Alexander McQueen suits to brunch and attend the opera with a priceless antique diamond necklace decorating her cleavage. "He's been coming in to buy cupcakes for quite some time. We go to lunch. It's not that big of a mystery."

Did it seem like a mystery to others? A lick of panic curled through her stomach. She couldn't ruin this for Jonas. If other people got suspicious because she wasn't the type of woman a billionaire CEO should want to marry, then everything might fall apart.

Breathe. He'd made that decision. Not her. He'd picked Viv and anyone who thought she wasn't good enough for him could jump in a lake.

"But he married you." Grace clapped her hands, eyes twinkling. "Tell us how he proposed, what you wore at the wedding. Ooooh, show us pictures."

Since his proposal had begun with the line "This is going to sound crazy, but hear me out," Viv avoided that subject by holding out her left hand to dazzle her sisters with the huge diamond and then grabbing her phone to thumb up the shots Warren had taken at Jonas's request. The yellow of her dress popped next to Jonas's dark suit and they made an incredibly striking couple if she did say so herself. Mostly because she had the best-looking husband on the planet, so no one even noticed her.

"Is that Hendrix Harris in the shot?" Hope sniffed and the disapproval on her face spoke volumes against the man whose picture graced local gossip rags on a regular basis.

"Jonas and Hendrix are friends," Viv said mildly as she flipped through a few more pictures that mercifully did not include North Carolina's biggest scandalmonger. "They went to Duke together. I'll try not to let him corrupt me if we socialize."

As far as she could tell, Hendrix had scarcely noticed her at the wedding, and he'd seemed preoccupied at the cocktail lounge where they'd gone to have drinks after the ceremony. The man was pretty harmless.

"Just be careful," Hope implored her, smoothing an invisible wrinkle from her skirt. "You married Jonas so quickly and it appears as if he may have some unsavory associations. I say this with love, but you haven't demonstrated a great track record when it comes to the men you fall for."

That shouldn't have cut so deeply. It was true. But still.

"What Hope means is that you tend to leap before you look, Viv," Grace corrected, her eyes rolling in their sister's direction, but only Viv could see the show of support. It soothed the ragged places inside that Hope's comment had made. A little.

"It's not a crime to be passionate about someone." Hands on her hips, Viv surveyed the three women, none of whom seemed to remember what it was like to be single and alone. "But for your information, Jonas and I were friends first. We share common interests. He gives me advice about my business. We have a solid foundation to build on."

"Oh." Hope processed that. "I didn't realize you were being so practical about this. I'm impressed that you managed to marry a man without stars in your eyes. That's a relief."

Great. She'd gotten the seal of approval from Hope solely because she'd skirted the truth with a bland recitation of unromantic facts about her marriage. Her heart clenched. That was the opposite of what she wanted. But this was the marriage she had, the one she could handle. For now. Tomorrow, Jonas would take her to his father's house to meet his grandfather and she hoped to "practice" being married a whole lot more.

Thankfully, she'd kept Jonas in the dark about her feelings. If he could kiss her like he had last night and not figure out that she'd been this close to melting into a little puddle, she could easily snow his family with a few public displays of affection.

It was behind closed doors that she was worried about. That's where she feared she might forget that her marriage was fake. And as she'd just been unceremoniously reminded, she had a tendency to get serious way too fast, which in her experience was a stellar way to get a man to start looking for the exit.

That was the part that hurt the most. She wanted to care about someone, to let him know he was her whole world and have him say that in return. It wasn't neediness. She wasn't being clingy. That's what love looked like to her and she refused to believe otherwise.

But she'd yet to find a man who agreed with her, and Jonas was no exception. They had a deal and she would stick to it.

The house Jonas had grown up in lay on the outskirts of Raleigh in an upscale neighborhood that was homey and unpretentious. Jonas's father, who had changed his name to Brian when he became a legal US citizen upon marrying his American wife, hadn't gone into the family business, choosing to become a professor at Duke University instead.

That had left a hole in the Kim empire, one Jonas had gladly filled. He and Grandfather got along well, likely because they were so similar. They both had a drive to succeed, a natural professionalism and a sense of honor that harbored trust in others who did business with Kim Electronics.

Though they corresponded nearly every day in some electronic form, the time difference prevented them from speaking often, and an in-person visit was even rarer. The last time Jonas had seen Grandfather had been during a trip to Seoul for a board meeting about eighteen months ago. He'd invited his parents to come with him, as they hadn't visited Korea in several years.

"Are you nervous?" Jonas glanced over at Viv, who had clutched her hands together in her lap the second the car had hit Glenwood Avenue. Her knuckles couldn't get any whiter.

"Oh, God. You can tell," she wailed. "I was trying so hard to be cool."

He bit back a grin and passed a slow-moving minivan. "Viv, they're just people. I promise they will like you."

"I'm not worried about that. Everyone likes me, especially after I give them cupcakes," she informed him loftily.

There was a waxed paper box at her feet on the floorboard that she'd treated as carefully as a newborn baby. When he'd reached for it, she'd nearly taken his hand off at the wrist, telling him in no uncertain terms the cupcakes were for her new family. Jonas was welcome to come by Cupcaked next week and pick out whatever he wanted, but the contents of that box were off-limits.

He kind of liked Bossy Viv. Of course he liked Sweet Viv, Uncertain Viv, Eager-to-Help Viv. He'd seen plenty of new facets in the last week since they'd moved in together, more than he'd have expected given that they'd known each other so long. It was fascinating.

"What are you worried about then?" he asked.

"You know good and well." Without warning, she slid a hand over his thigh and squeezed. Fire rocketed up his leg and scored his groin, nearly doubling him over with the sudden and unexpected need.

Only his superior reflexes kept the Mercedes on the road. But he couldn't stop the curse that flew from his mouth.

"Sorry," he muttered but she didn't seem bothered by his language.

"See, you're just as bad as me." Her tone was laced with irony. "All that practice and we're even jumpier than we were before."

Because the practice had ended before he started peeling off her clothes. Ironic how his marriage of convenience meant his wife was right there in his house—conveniently located in the bedroom next to his. He could hear her moving around between the walls and sometimes, he lay awake at night listening for the slightest movement to indicate she was likewise awake, aching to try one of those kisses with a lot less fabric in the way.

That kind of need was so foreign to him that he wasn't handling it well.

"I'm not jumpy," he lied. "I'm just…"

Frustrated.

There was no good way to finish that sentence without opening up a conversation about changing their relationship into something that it wasn't supposed to be. An annulment was so much less sticky than a divorce, though he'd finally accepted that he was using that as an excuse.

The last thing he could afford to do was give in to the simmering awareness between them. Jonas had convinced himself it was easy to honor the pact because he really didn't feel much when it came to relationships. Sure, he enjoyed sex, but it had always been easy to walk away when the woman pushed for more.

With Viv, the spiral of heat and need was dizzyingly strong. He felt too much, and Marcus's experience was like a big neon sign, reminding him that it was better never to go down that path. What was he supposed to do, stop being friends with Viv if things went haywire between them? Neither was there a good way to end their relationship before the merger.

So he was stuck. He couldn't act on his sudden and fierce longing to pull this car over into a shadowy bower of oak trees and find out if all of Viv tasted like sugar and spice and everything nice.

"Maybe we shouldn't touch each other," he suggested.

That was a good solution. Except for the part where they were married. Married people touched each other. He bit back the nasty word that had sprung to his lips. Barely.

"Oh." She nodded. "If you think that won't cause problems, sure."

Of course it was going to cause problems. He nearly groaned. But the problems had nothing to do with what she assumed. "Stop being so reasonable. I'm pulling you away from your life with very little compensation in return. You should be demanding and difficult."

Brilliant. He'd managed to make it sound like touching her was one of the compensation methods. He really needed to get out of this car now that he had a hyperawareness of how easily she could— and would—reach out to slide a hand full of questing fingers into his lap.

Viv grinned and crossed her arms, removing that possibility. "In that case, I'm feeling very bereft in the jewelry department, Mr. Kim. As your wife, I should be draped in gems, don't you think?"

"Absolutely." What did it say about how messed up he was that the way *Mr. Kim* rolled off her tongue turned him on? "Total oversight on my part. Which I will rectify immediately."

The fourteen-carat diamond on her finger was on loan from a guy Jonas knew in the business, though the hefty fee he'd paid to procure it could have bought enough bling to blind her. Regardless, if Viv wanted jewelry, that's what she'd get.

They drove into his parents' neighborhood right on time and he parked in the long drive that led to the house. "Ready?"

She nodded. "All that talk about jewelry got me over my nerves. Thanks."

That made one of them.

His mom opened the door before they'd even hit

the stone steps at the entryway, likely because she'd been watching for the car. But instead of engulfing Jonas in the first of what would be many hugs, she ignored her only child in favor of her new daughter-in-law.

"You must be Viviana," his mother gushed, and swept Viv up in an embrace that was part friendly and part *Thank you, God, I finally have a daughter.* "I'm so happy to meet you."

Viv took it in stride. "Hi, Mrs. Kim. I'm happy to meet you, too. Please call me Viv."

Of course she wasn't ruffled. There was so little that seemed to trip her up—except when Jonas touched her. All practicing had done was create surprisingly acute sexual tension that even a casual observer would recognize as smoldering awareness.

He was currently pretending it didn't exist. Because that would make it not so, right?

"Hi, Mom," he threw in blithely since she hadn't even glanced in his direction.

"Your grandfather is inside. He'd like to talk to you while I get to know Viviana. Tell me everything," she said to her new daughter-in-law as she accepted the box of cupcakes with a smile. "Have you started thinking about kids yet?"

Jonas barely bit back another curse. "Mom, please. We just got here. Viv doesn't need the third degree about personal stuff."

Right out of the gate with the baby questions? Really? He'd expected a little decorum from his mom.

In vain, obviously, and a mistake because he hadn't had a chance to go over that with Viv. Should they say they didn't want children? That she couldn't have any?

He and Viv clearly should have spent less time "practicing" and more in deep conversation about all aspects of potential questions that might come up this weekend. Which they'd have to rectify tonight before going to bed. In the same room.

His mother shot him a glare. "Grandchildren are not personal. The hope of one day getting some is the only reason I keep you around, after all."

That made Viv laugh, which delighted his mother, so really, there was nothing left to do but throw up his hands and go seek out Grandfather for his own version of the third degree.

Grandfather held court in the Kim living room, talking to his son. The older Jonas's dad got, the more he resembled Grandfather, but the similarities ended there. Where Brian Kim had adopted an American name to match his new homeland, Kim Jung-Su wore his Korean heritage like the badge of honor it was.

Kim Electronics had been born after the war, during a boom in Korean capitalism that only a select few had wisely taken advantage of. Jonas loved his dad, but Grandfather had been his mentor, his partner as Jonas had taken what Jung-Su had built and expanded it into the critical US market. They'd created a chaebol, a family-run conglomerate, where none had existed, and they'd done it together.

And he was about to lie to his grandfather's face solely to avoid marrying a disaster of a woman who might cause the Kim family shame.

It was a terrible paradox and not for the first time he heard Warren's voice of reason in his head asking why he couldn't just tell Grandfather the truth. But then he remembered that Sun's grandfather and Jonas's grandfather had fought in the war together and were closer than brothers. Jonas refused to out Sun and her unsuitable lover strictly for his own benefit. No, this way was easier.

And it wasn't a lie. He and Viv were married. That was all anyone needed to know.

Grandfather greeted Jonas in Korean and then switched to English as a courtesy since he was in an English-speaking house. "You are looking well."

"As are you." Jonas bowed to show his respect and then hugged his dad, settling in next to him on the couch. "It's a pleasure to see you."

Grandfather arched a thick brow. "An unexpected pleasure I assume? I wanted to meet your new wife personally. To welcome her into the family."

"She is very honored. Mom waylaid her or she'd be here to meet you, as well."

"I asked your mother to. I wanted to speak with you privately."

As if it had been some prearranged signal, Jonas's dad excused himself and the laser sights of

Jung-Su had zero distractions. The temperature of the room shot up about a thousand degrees. One misstep and the whole plan would come crashing down. And Jonas suddenly hated the idea of losing this tenuous link with Viv, no matter how precarious that link was.

"Now, then." Grandfather steepled his hands together and smiled. "I'm very pleased you have decided to marry. It is a big step that will bring you many years of happiness. Belated congratulations."

Jonas swallowed his surprise. What was the wily old man up to? He'd expected a cross-examination designed to uncover the plot that Grandfather surely suspected. "Thank you. Your approval means a lot to me."

"As a wedding gift, I'd like to give you the Kim ancestral home."

"What? I mean, that's a very generous gesture, Grandfather." And crafty, as the property in question lay outside of Seoul, seven thousand miles away from North Carolina. Jonas couldn't refuse or Grandfather would be insulted. But there was an angle here that Jonas couldn't quite work out.

"Of course I'd hoped you'd live in it with Sun Park, but I understand that you cannot curb the impulses of the heart."

Jonas stared at his grandfather as if he'd suddenly started speaking Klingon. The impulses of the heart? That was the exact opposite of the impression he'd wanted to convey. Sure, he'd hoped to convince everyone that they were a couple, but only so that no one's suspicions were aroused. Solid and unbreakable would be more to his liking when describing his marriage, not *impulsive* and certainly not because he'd fallen madly in love.

This was the worst sort of twist. Never would he have thought he'd be expected to sell his marriage as a love match. Was that something that he and Viv were going to have to practice, too? His stomach twisted itself inside out. How the hell was he supposed to know what love looked like?

Regardless of the curveball, it was the confirmation Jonas had been looking for. Grandfather was on board with Viv, and Jonas had cleared the first hurdle after receiving that ominous text message the other day. "I'm glad you understand. I've been seeing Viv for almost a year and I simply couldn't imagine marrying anyone else."

That much at least was true, albeit a careful hedge about the nature of his intentions toward Viv during that year. And thankfully they'd become good enough friends that he felt comfortable asking her to help him avoid exactly what he'd suspected Grandfather had in mind. Apparently throwing Sun in his path *had* been an attempt to get Jonas to Korea more often, if not permanently. It was counter to Jonas's long-term strategy, the one he still hadn't brought to Grandfather because the merger hadn't happened yet. Once Park Industries and Kim Electronics became one, they could leverage the foothold Jonas had already built in America by moving the headquarters to North Carolina, yet keep manufacturing in Korea under the Park branch.

It was also the opportune time to pass the reins, naming Jonas the CEO of the entire operation. The dominoes were in much better position now, thanks to the huge bullet Viv had helped him dodge without upsetting anyone. It was…everything.

Grandfather chatted for a few more minutes about his plans while in the US, including a request for a tour of the Kim Building, and then asked Jonas to introduce him to Viv.

He found her in the kitchen writing down her cupcake recipe for his mother.

"You got her secret recipe already, Mom?" Jonas asked with a laugh. "I guess I don't have to ask whether everyone is getting along."

His mother patted his arm. "You obviously underestimate how much your wife cares for you. I didn't even have to ask twice."

Viv blushed and it was so pretty on her, he couldn't tear his gaze from her face all at once, even though he was speaking to his mom. "On the contrary, I'm quite aware of how incredibly lucky I am that Viv married me."

"You didn't have to ask me *that* twice either," Viv pointed out. "Apparently I lack the ability to say no to anyone with the name Kim."

An excellent point that he really wished she hadn't brought up on the heels of his discovery of how much he enjoyed it when she called him Mr. Kim. All at once, a dozen suggestions designed to get her to say yes over and over sprang to his lips. But with his mom's keen-eyed gaze cutting between the two of them, he needed to get himself under control immediately.

"Come and say hi to my grandfather," he said instead, and she nodded eagerly.

She was far too good to him. For the first time, it bothered him. What was she getting out of this farce? Some advice about how to run her business? That had seemed inadequate before they'd gotten married. Now? It was nearly insulting how little he was doing for her.

She had to have another reason for being here. And all at once, he wanted to know what it was.

Four

Ten minutes into dinner, Jonas figured out his grandfather's angle. The wily old man was trying to drive him insane with doubt about pulling off this ruse, especially now that he had *impulses of the heart* echoing through his head. Jonas was almost dizzy from trying to track all the verbal land mines that might or might not be strewn through random conversational openers.

Even "pass the butter" had implications. Grandfather hated butter.

And if Grandfather failed at putting Jonas in the loony bin, Viv was doing her part to finish the job, sitting next to him looking fresh and beautiful as she reminded him on a second-by-second basis that she was well within touching distance. Not just easily accessible. But *available* to be touched. It was *expected*. Would a loving husband sling his arm across the back of her chair? Seemed reasonable.

But the moment he did it as he waited for his mom to serve the kimchi stew she'd made in honor of Grandfather's visit, Viv settled into the crook of his elbow, which had not been his intent at all. She fit so well, he couldn't help but let his arm relax so that it fully embraced her and somehow his fingers ended up doing this little dance down her bare arm, testing whether the silkiness felt as good all the way down as it did near her shoulder.

It did.

"...don't you think, Jonas?"

Blinking, Jonas tore his attention away from his wife's skin and focused on his dad. "Sure. I definitely think so."

"That's great," Brian said with a nod and a wink. "It wasn't a stretch to think you'd be on board."

Fantastic. What in the world had he just agreed to that had his father winking, of all things? Jonas pulled his arm from around Viv's shoulders. At this point, it seemed like everyone was convinced they were a couple and all the touching had done nothing but distract him.

Viv leaned in, her hand resting on his thigh. It was dangerously close to being in his lap. One small shift would do it, and his muscles strained to repeat the experience. But before he could sort her intention, she murmured in his ear, "We're playing Uno later. As a team. You'll have to teach me."

Card games with a hard-on. That sounded like the opposite of fun. But at least he knew what he'd absently agreed to, and shot Viv a grateful smile. Her return smile did all sorts of things that it shouldn't have, not the least of which was give him the sense that they were coconspirators. They were in this farce together and he appreciated that more than he could say. At least they could laugh about this later. Or something.

Grandfather was watching him closely as he spooned up a bite of stew, and Jonas braced for the next round of insanity. Sure enough, Grandfather cleared his throat.

"Will you and your bride be starting a family soon?"

Not this again and from his grandfather, too? Obviously Jonas's mother had a vested interest in the answer strictly because she wanted babies to spoil, but Grandfather wasn't asking for anything close to that reason. It was all part of the test.

"Not soon," he hedged because family was important to the Kims. It was a source of frustration for both his parents and his grandparents that they'd only had one child apiece, and Jonas imagined they'd all be thrilled if he said Viv wanted a dozen. "Viv owns a bakery and it's doing very well. She'd like to focus on her career for a while."

Yes. That was the reason they weren't having kids

right away. Why had he been racking his brain over that? Except now he was thinking about the conversation where he had to tell everyone that while he cared about Viv, they were better as friends, so the marriage was over. While it soothed his sense of honor that it was the truth, he'd never considered that the annulment would upset his family.

"We're having her cupcakes for dessert," his mother threw in with a beaming smile. "They look scrumptious."

Perfect segue and took some heat off a subject that Jonas suddenly did not want to contemplate. "The lemon are my favorite. One bite and that was when I decided I couldn't let Viv get away."

The adoring glance she shot him thumped him in the gut. The little secret smile playing about her lips worked in tandem, spreading tendrils of heat through him in ways that should be uncomfortable at a table full of Kims who were all watching him closely. But the sensation was too enjoyable to squelch.

"Honestly, that was when I knew he was special," Viv admitted, and Jonas nearly did a double take at the wistful note in her voice. "He appreciates my cupcakes in a way regular customers don't. A lot goes into the recipes and I don't just mean my time. It's a labor of love, born out of a desire to make people happy, and I can see on his face that I've done that. Most customers just devour the thing without stopping to breathe, but Jonas always takes one bite and immediately stops to savor it. Then he tells me how great it is before taking another bite."

Well, yeah, because he could taste the sunshine in it, as if she'd somehow condensed a few rays and woven them through the ingredients. How could he not take his time to fully appreciate the unique experience of a Viviana Dawson cupcake?

Jonas blinked, dragging his lids down over his suddenly dry eyes. He didn't do that *every* time, not the way she was describing it, as if a cupcake held all that meaning.

He glanced at his mom, who looked a little misty.

"That sounds like a magical courtship," she said.

"Oh, it was," Viv agreed enthusiastically. "It was like one of those movies where the hero pretends he only wants the cupcakes when he comes into the shop, but it's really to see the baker. But I always knew from the first that the way to his heart was through my frosting."

His mother laughed and Jonas checked his eye roll because the whole point was to sell this nonsense. Everyone was eating it up, no pun intended, so why mess with the ridiculous story Viv was spinning?

Except the whole thing made him uncomfortable.

Surely his grandfather wouldn't appreciate hearing his successor described with such romanticism. If anything, Viv could help Jonas's case by telling everyone how hard he worked and how difficult it was to pry him away from his cell phone when they went to lunch.

He sighed. She couldn't say that. It would be a big, fat lie. When he did anything with Viv, he always switched his phone to do not disturb. He loved listening to stories about her sisters, or a new recipe she was working through. But it didn't mean he was gaga over her like a besotted fool.

Yet…that's what he needed his grandfather to buy, as difficult as it was to envision. Grandfather hadn't accepted Jonas's marriage to Viv because she'd helped him increase profits or created an advantageous business alliance. Viv was an *impulse of the heart*.

How had he gotten caught in the middle of trying to prove to his grandfather that Jonas was a committed, solid CEO candidate, while also attempting to convince him that he and Viv had fallen in love? And Jonas had no illusions about the necessity of maintaining the current vibe, not after his grandfather smiled over Viv's enthusiastic retelling of what would probably forever be called the Cupcake Courtship. It was madness.

"Will you bring your wife to Seoul to visit the Kim ancestral home?" Grandfather asked in the lull. "It's yours now. Perhaps you'll want to redecorate?"

Jonas nearly groaned. He hadn't had four seconds to mention the gift to Viv. Her eyebrows lifted in silent question and he blessed her discretion.

"We're actually looking for a house together in Raleigh," Jonas improvised much more smoothly than he would have guessed he could. Viv's eyebrows did another reach-for-the-sky move as he rushed on. "So probably we won't make it to Korea anytime soon. But we do both appreciate the gift."

Nothing like a good reminder that Jonas's home was in America. The future of the company lay here, not in Seoul. The more he could root himself in North Carolina, the better. Of course the answer was to buy a property here. With Viv. A new ancestral home in North Carolina. Then his statement to his grandfather wouldn't be a lie.

"Yes, thank you so much, Mr. Kim," Viv said sweetly. "We'll discuss our work schedules and find a mutual time we can travel. I would be honored to see your ancestral home. Mrs. Kim, perhaps you'd advise me on whether the decor needs refurbishing?"

Jonas's mom smiled so widely that it was a wonder she didn't crack her face. "That's a lovely idea. I would be thrilled to go to lunch and discuss the house, as I've always loved the locale."

Speechless, Jonas watched the exchange with a very real sense of his life sliding out of control and no way to put on the brakes. In the last two minutes, he'd managed to rope himself into shopping for a house in Raleigh, then traveling to Korea so Viv could visit Seoul with the express intent of redecorating a house neither of them wanted...with his mom. What next?

"While you're in Korea," Grandfather said, and his tone was so leading that everyone's head turned toward him, "we should discuss taking next steps toward increasing your responsibilities at Kim Electronics. The board will look very favorably on how you've matured, Jonas. Your accomplishments with the American market are impressive. I would be happy to recommend you as the next CEO when I retire."

The crazy train screeched to a halt in the dead center of Are You Kidding Me Station. *Say something. Tell him you're honored.*

But Jonas's throat froze as his brain tried to sort through his grandfather's loaded statements.

Everything he'd worked for had just been handed to him on a silver platter—that Viv was holding in her delicate fingers. The implications were staggering. Grandfather liked that Jonas was married. It was a huge wrinkle he had never seen coming.

Now he couldn't annul the marriage or he'd risk losing Grandfather's approval with the board. How was he supposed to tell Viv that the favor he'd asked of her had just been extended by about a year?

And what did it mean that his insides were doing a secret dance of happiness at getting to keep Viv longer than planned?

The spare bedroom lay at the end of a quiet hall and had its own en suite bathroom. Nice. Viv wasn't too keen on the idea of wandering around in her bathrobe. At least not outside the bedroom. Inside was another story.

Because Jonas was on this side of the closed door. Time to ramp it up.

If she hoped to build her confidence with a man, there was no better scenario to play that out than this one, especially since she already knew they were attracted to each other And headed for a divorce. None of this was real, so she could practice without fear.

She shivered as her gorgeous husband loosened his tie and threw himself onto the bed with a groan. *Shivered.* What was that but a commentary on this whole situation?

"Bad day, sweetie?" she deadpanned, carefully keeping her voice light. But holy cow, Jonas was so sexy with his shirtsleeves rolled up and his bare feet crossed at the ankle as he tossed an elbow over his eyes.

"That was one of the most difficult dinners I've ever endured," he confessed, as if there was nothing odd about being in a bedroom together with the door closed, while he lounged on the bed looking like a commercial for something sensual and expensive.

"Your family is great." She eased onto the bed because she wanted to and she could. It wasn't like there were a ton of other seats in the cute little bedroom. Well, except for the matching chairs near the bay window that flanked an inlaid end table. But she didn't want to sit way over there when the centerpiece of the room lay on the bed.

As the mattress shifted under her weight, he peeked out from beneath his elbow, his dark eyes seeking hers. "You're only saying that to be nice. You should stage a fight and go home. It would serve me right to have to stay here and field questions about the stability of our marriage."

As if she'd ever do that when the best part of this fake marriage had just started. She was sharing a bedroom with Jonas Kim and he was her husband and the night was rife with possibilities.

There came the shiver again and it was delicious. *Careful.*

This was the part where she always messed up with men by seeming too eager. Messing up with Jonas was not happening. There was no do-over.

Of course, scoring with Jonas had its issues, too. Like the fact that she couldn't keep him. This was just practice, she reminded herself. That was the only way she could get it together.

"I'm not staging a fight." She shook her head and risked reaching out to stroke Jonas's hair in a totally casual gesture meant to soothe him, because after all, he did seem pretty stressed. "What would we fight about? Money?"

"I don't know. No." The elbow came off his face and he let his eyes drift closed as she ran her fingers over his temples. "That feels nice. You don't have to do that."

Oh, yes. She did. This was her chance to touch Jonas in a totally innocuous way and study her husband's body while he wasn't aware.

"It's possible for me to do something because I want to instead of out of a sense of obligation, you know."

He chuckled. "Point taken. I'm entirely too sensitive to how big a favor this is and how difficult navigating my family can be."

Stroking his hair might go down as one of the greatest pleasures of her life. It was soft and silky and thick. The inky strands slid across her fingertips as she buried them deep and rubbed lightly against his scalp, which earned her a groan that was amazingly sexy.

"Relax," she murmured, and was only half talking to herself as her insides contracted. "I don't find your family difficult. Your mom is great and I don't know if you know this or not, but your grandfather does not in fact breathe fire."

"He gave us a house." His eyes popped open and he glanced over at her, shrinking the slight distance between them. "There are all sorts of underlying expectations associated with that, not the least of which is how upset he's going to be when I have to give it back."

She shrugged, pretending like it wasn't difficult to get air into her lungs when he focused on her so intently. "Don't give it back. Keep it and we'll go visit, like we promised."

"Viv." He sat up, taking his beautiful body out of reach, which was a shame. "You're being entirely too accommodating. Were you not listening to the conversation at dinner? This is only going to get more complicated the longer we drag it out. And we *are* going to be dragging it out apparently."

Normally, this would be where she threw herself prostrate at a man's feet and wept with joy over the fact that he wasn't calling things off. But she wasn't clingy anymore. Newly Minted Independent Viv needed to play this a whole different way if she wanted to get to a place where she had a man slavishly devoted to her. And she would not apologize for wishing for a man who loved her so much that he would never dream of calling the duration of their marriage "dragging it out."

"You say that like being married to me is a chore," she scolded lightly. "I was listening at dinner. I heard the words *CEO* and *Jonas* in the same sentence. Did you? Because that sounded good to me."

"It is good. For me. Not you. I'm now essentially in the position of using you to further my career goals for an extended period of time. Not just until the merger happens. But until my grandfather retires and fully transitions the role of CEO to me. That could take months. A year."

Oh, God. A whole year of living with Jonas in his amazing loft and being his wife? That was a lot of practicing for something that would never be real. How could she possibly hide her feelings for Jonas that long? Worse, they'd probably grow stronger the longer she stayed in his orbit. How fair was it to keep torturing herself like this?

On the flip side, she'd promised to do this for Jonas as a favor. As a *friend*. He wasn't interested in more or he'd have told her. Practice was all she could reasonably expect from this experience. It had to be enough.

"That's a significant development, no doubt. But I don't feel used. And I'm not going anywhere."

Jonas scowled instead of overflowing with gratitude. "I can't figure out what you're getting out of this. It was already a huge sacrifice, even when it was only for a few weeks until my grandfather got his deal going with Park. Now this. Are you dying of cancer or something?"

She forced a laugh but there was nothing funny about his assumptions. Or the fact that she didn't have a good answer for why she didn't hate the idea of sticking around as long as Jonas would have her. Maybe there was something wrong with that, but it was her business, not his. "What, like I'm trying to check off everything on my bucket list before I die and being married to Jonas Kim was in the top three? That's a little arrogant, don't you think?"

When he flinched, she almost took it back, but that's how Newly Minted Viv rolled. The last thing he needed to hear was that being married to him occupied the top spot on all her lists. And on that note, it was definitely time to put a few more logs on the pile before she set it on fire.

"Running a cupcake business is hard," she told him firmly. "You've built Kim Electronics from the ground up. You should know how it is. You work seventy hours a week and barely make a dent. Who has time for a relationship? But I get lonely, same as anyone. This deal is perfect for me because we can hang out with no pressure. I like you. Is that so hard to believe?"

Good. Deflect. Give him just enough truth to make it plausible.

His face relaxed into an easy grin. "Only a little. I owe you so much. Not sure my scintillating personality makes up for being stuck sharing a bedroom with me."

"Yeah, that part sucks, all right," she murmured, and let her gaze trail down his body. What better way to "practice" being less clingy than to get good and needy and then force herself to walk away? "We should use this opportunity to get a little more comfortable with each other."

The atmosphere got intense as his expression darkened, and she could tell the idea intrigued him.

"What? Why? We've already sold the coupledom story to my family. It's a done deal and went way better than I was expecting. We don't have to do the thing where we touch each other anymore."

Well, that stung. She'd had the distinct impression he liked touching her.

"Oh, I wish that was true." She stuck an extra tinge of dismay into her tone, just to be sure it was really clear that she wasn't panting after him. Even though she was lying through her teeth. "But we still have all of tomorrow with your family. And you're planning to meet mine, right? We have to sell that we're hopelessly in love all over again. I'm really concerned about tongues wagging. After all, Joy's husband knows everyone who's anyone. The business world is small."

Jonas's eyes went a little wide. "We just have to sell being married. No one said anything about love."

"But that's why people get married, Jonas." Something flickered through his expression that looked a lot like panic. And it set a bunch of gears in motion in her head. Maybe they should be using this time to get matters straight instead of doing a lot of touching. Because all at once, she was really curious about an important aspect of this deal that she'd thus far failed to question. "Don't you think so?"

"That people should only get married if they're in love? I don't know." But he shifted his gaze away so quickly that it was obvious he had something going on inside. "I've never been married before."

That was a careful way to answer the question. Did that mean he had been in love but not enough to marry the girl? Or he'd never been in love? Maybe he was nursing a serious broken heart and it was too painful to discuss. "Your parents are married. Aren't they in love?"

"Sure. It's just not something I've given a lot of thought to."

"So think about it." She was pushing him, plain and simple, but this was important compatibility stuff that she'd never questioned. Everyone believed in love. Right? "I'm just wondering now why you needed a fake wife. Maybe you should have been looking for someone to fall in love with this whole time instead of taking me to lunch for a year."

He hadn't been dating anyone, this she knew for a fact because she'd asked. Multiple times. Her curiosity on the matter might even be described as morbid.

"Viv." His voice had gone quiet and she liked the way he said her name with so much texture. "If I'd wanted to spend time with someone other than you over the last year, I would have. I like you. Is that so hard to believe?"

Her mouth curved up before she could catch it. But why should she? Jonas made her smile, even when he was deflecting her question. Probably because he didn't think about her "that way" no matter how hot the kiss outside her bedroom had been. One-sided then. They were friends. Period. And she should definitely not be sad about that. He was a wonderful, kind man who made not thinking wicked thoughts impossible the longer they sat on a bed together behind closed doors.

Yeah, she could pretend she was practicing for a relationship with some other man all she wanted. Didn't change the fact that deep in her heart Viv wished she could be the person Jonas would fall madly in love with.

But she knew she couldn't keep Jonas. At least she was in the right place to fix her relationship pitfalls.

Now, how did one go about seducing a man while giving him the distinct impression she could take him or leave him?

Five

The bed in Jonas's mother's guest room must have razor blades sewn into the comforter. It was the only explanation for why his skin felt like it was on fire as he forced himself to lie there chatting with Viv as if they really were a real married couple having a debrief after his family's third degree.

They *were* a real married couple having a chat.

If only she hadn't brought up the *L* word. The one concept he had zero desire to talk about when it came to marriage. Surely Viv knew real married couples who didn't love each other. It couldn't be that huge of a departure, otherwise the divorce rate would be a lot lower.

But they were a married couple, albeit not a tra-

ditional one behind closed doors. If they were a traditional married couple, Jonas would be sliding his
fingers across the mattress and taking hold of Viv's
thigh so he could brace her for the exploration to
come. His lips would fit so well in the hollow near
her throat. So far, she hadn't seemed to clue in that
every muscle beneath his skin strained toward her,
and he had no idea how she wasn't as affected by the
sizzling awareness as he was.

They were on a bed. They were married. The
door was closed. What did that equal? Easy math—
and it was killing him that they were getting it so
wrong. Why wasn't he rolling his wife beneath him
and getting frisky with breathless anticipation as
they shushed each other before someone heard them
through the walls?

"Since we like each other so much, maybe we
should talk about the actual sleeping arrangements,"
she suggested. "There's not really a good way to
avoid sharing the bed and we're keeping things platonic when no one's around."

Oh, right, because this was an exercise in insanity, just like dinner. He really shouldn't be picturing
Viv sliding between cool sheets, naked of course,
and peeking up at him from under her lashes as she
clutched the pale blue fabric to her breasts.

"I can sleep on the floor," he croaked. She
cocked a brow, eyeing him as if she could see right
through his zipper to the hard-on he wasn't hiding

very well. "I insist. You're doing me a favor. It's the least I can do."

"I wasn't expecting anyone to sleep on the floor. We're friends. We can sleep in the same bed and keep our hands off each other. Right?" Then she blinked and something happened to her eyes. Her gaze deepened, elongating the moment, and heat teased along the edges of his nerve endings. "Unless you think it would be too much of a temptation."

He swallowed. Was she a mind reader now? How had she figured out that he had less than pure thoughts about sharing a bed with his wife? How easy it would be to reach out in the middle of the night, half-asleep, and pull her closer for a midnight kiss that wouldn't have any daylight consequences because nothing counted in the dark.

Except everything with Viv counted. That was the problem. They had a friendship he didn't want to lose and he had taken a vow with Warren and Hendrix that he couldn't violate.

"No, of course not," he blurted out without checking his emphatic delivery. "I mean, definitely it'll be hard—" *Dear God.* "Nothing will be hard! Everything will be…" *Not easy. Don't say easy.* "I have to go check on…something."

Before he could fully internalize how much of an ass he was making of himself, he bolted from the bed and fled the room, calling over his shoulder, "Feel free to use the bathroom. I'll wait my turn."

Which was a shame because what he really

needed was a cold shower. Prowling around the house like a cat burglar because he didn't want to alert anyone he'd just kicked himself out of his own newlywed bedroom, Jonas poked around in his dad's study but felt like he was intruding in the hallowed halls of academia.

He and his dad were night and day. They loved each other, but Brian Kim wasn't a businessman in any way, shape or form. It was like the entrepreneurial gene had skipped a generation. Put Brian in a lecture hall and he was in his element. In truth, the only reason Jonas had gone to Duke was because his father was on faculty and his parents had gotten a discount on tuition. They'd refused to take a dime of Grandfather's money since Brian hadn't filled a position at Kim Electronics.

If his dad had taken a job at any other university, Jonas never would have met Warren, Hendrix and Marcus. His friendship with those guys had shaped his twenties, more so than he'd ever realized, until now.

The funeral had been brutal. So hard to believe his friend was inside that casket. His mom had held his hand the entire time and even as a twenty-one-year-old junior in college who desperately wanted to be hip, he hadn't let go once. Marcus had been down in the dumps for weeks, but they'd all shrugged it off. Typical male pride and bruised feelings. Who hadn't been the victim of a woman's fickle tastes?

But Marcus had been spiraling down and none of

them had seen it. That was the problem with love. It made you do crazy, out-of-character things. Like suicide.

Jonas slid into his dad's chair and swiveled it to face the window, letting the memory claw through his gut as he stared blindly at the koi pond outside in the garden. There was no shame in having missed the signs. Everyone had. But that reassurance rang as hollow today as it had ten years ago. What could he have done? Talked sense into the guy? Obviously the pain had been too great, and the lesson for Jonas was clear: don't let a woman get her hooks into you.

That was why he couldn't touch Viv anymore. The temptation wasn't just too much. It was deadly. Besides, she was his friend. He'd already crossed a bunch of lines in the name of ensuring his family bought into the marriage, but it was all just an excuse to have his cake and eat Viv, too.

Bad, bad thing to be thinking about. There was a part of him that couldn't believe Viv would be dangerous to his mental state. But the risks were too great, especially to their friendship. They'd gone a whole year without being tempted. What was different now? Proximity? Awareness? The fact that he'd already kissed her and couldn't undo the effect on his body every time he got within touching distance of her?

That one.

Sleeping with her in the bed was going to be torture. He really didn't know if he had it in him. Probably the best thing to do was sleep on the couch in the living room and set an alarm for something ridiculous like 5:00 a.m. Then he could go for a jog and come back like he'd slept in Viv's bed all night long. Of course he'd never jogged in his life…but he could start. Might burn off some of the awareness he couldn't shake.

That was the best plan. He headed back to the bedroom they shared to tell her.

But when he eased open the door and slipped inside, she was still in the bathroom. He settled onto the bed to wait, next to her open suitcase. There was literally no reason for him to glance inside other than it was right there. Open. With a frothy bunch of racy lingerie laid out across the other clothes.

Holy crap. Jonas's eyes burned the longer he stared at the thin straps and drapes of lace. Was that the *top*? Viv's breasts were supposed to be covered by that? Something that skimpy should be illegal. And red. But the lace was lemon yellow, the color of the frosting Viv slathered all over the cupcakes she always brought him when they had lunch. His mouth watered at the thought of tasting Viv through all that lace. It would be easy. The pattern would show 90 percent of her skin.

The little panties lay innocuously to the side as if an afterthought. Probably because there wasn't enough lace making up the bottom half of the outfit to rightfully call them panties. He could picture them perfectly on his wife's body and he could envision slowly stripping them off even more vividly.

Wait. What was Viv doing with such smoking-hot lingerie?

Was she planning to wear it for *him*? His brain had no ability to make sense of this revelation. She'd brought lingerie. To wear. Of course the only man in the vicinity was Jonas. Who else would she be wearing it for?

That was totally against the rules.

And totally against what he was capable of giving her in this marriage. She might as well drape herself in hearts and flowers. Viv clearly thought love was a recipe for marriage. Stir well and live happily ever after. He wasn't the right ingredient for that mix.

The sound of running water being shut off rattled through the walls. Viv had just emerged from the shower. He should get the hell out of that bedroom right now. But before he could stand, she walked out of the bathroom holding a towel loosely around her body. Her *naked* body. She was still wet. His gaze traced the line of one drop as it slid down her shoulder and disappeared behind the towel.

"Oh. I didn't know you'd come back," she announced unnecessarily as he was reasonably certain she wouldn't have waltzed into the room mostly naked if she'd known he was sitting on the bed.

"Sorry," he muttered, and meant to avert his eyes but the towel had slipped a little, which she'd done nothing to correct.

Maybe she wanted him to catch a glimpse of her perfect breasts. Not that he knew for sure that they were perfect. But the little half-moon slices peeking above the towel flashed at him more brightly than a neon sign, and his whole body went up in flames.

Anything that powerful at only a quarter strength had to be perfect in its entirety.

"Did you want to take a turn in the bathroom?" she asked casually. Still standing there. Wet. In a towel. Naked.

"Uh, sure." He didn't stand. He should cross the room and barricade himself in the bathroom, where it wouldn't matter if she'd used all the hot water because the shower needed to be glacial.

"Okay. Can you give me two minutes? I need to dry my hair." And then she laughed with a little peal that punched him the gut. "Normally I would wrap it up in the towel but there are only two and I didn't want to hog them all."

Then she pulled on the edge of the towel, loosening it from the column it formed around her body and lifted the tail end to the ends of her dripping hair. A long slice of skin peeked through the opening she'd unwittingly created and the answering flash of heat that exploded in his groin would have put him on his knees if he'd been standing. Good thing he hadn't moved.

"You should get dressed," he suggested, but she didn't hear him because his voice wasn't working. Besides, *dressed* could have a lot of different meanings, and the frothy yellow concoction in her suitcase appeared to be the next outfit of choice. If she hadn't been planning to slip it on, it wouldn't be on top, laid out so carefully.

Oh, man. Would she have been wearing it when he got into bed later? No warning, just bam!

He should pretend he hadn't seen the yellow concoction. How else could he find out if that had been her plan? That had to be her plan. Please, God, let it be her plan.

He was so hard, it was a wonder his erection hadn't busted out of his zipper.

Clearing his throat, he tested out speaking again. "I can come back."

That, she heard. "Oh, you don't have to. Really, I've taken way too long already. We're sharing and I'm not used to that. The shower was lovely and I couldn't help standing there under the spray, just letting my mind drift."

Great. Now his mind was drifting—into the shower with her as she stood there. Naked. Letting the water sluice down her body, eyes closed with a small, rapturous smile gracing her face.

He groaned. What was he doing to himself?

"Are you okay?" Her attention honed in on him and she apparently forgot she wasn't wearing anything but a damp towel because she immediately crossed the room to loom over him, her expression laced with concern.

It would take less than a second to reach out and

snag her by the waist, pulling her down into his lap. That towel would fall, revealing her perfect breasts, and they'd be right there, ripe and available to taste. No yellow concoction needed. But that would be criminal. She should get to wear her newlywed lingerie if she wanted.

"Oh." Viv blushed all at once, the pink stain spreading across her cheeks, and Jonas could not tear his eyes off her face. But she was staring at the open suitcase. "You didn't see that ridiculous thing Grace gave me, did you?"

She picked up the yellow lacy top and held it up to her body, draping it over the towel one-handed, which had the immediate consequence of smooshing her breasts higher. "Can you imagine me wearing this?"

With absolute, brilliant clarity.

"I don't know what she was thinking," Viv continued as if his entire body wasn't poised to explode. "'Open this with Jonas,' she says with a sly wink. I thought it was going to be a joke, like a gravy boat, and besides, this isn't a real marriage, so I didn't think you'd actually want to help open gifts. Sorry I didn't wait for you."

She rolled her eyes with another laugh that did not help things down below.

"That's okay. Next time." What was he saying? *Sure, I'll help open future gifts full of shockingly transparent clothing that would make a porn star blush?* "Your sister meant well. She doesn't know we're not sleeping together."

Or rather they weren't yet. In a scant few minutes, they'd be in the bed. Together. Maybe some sleeping would occur but it wasn't looking too likely unless he got his body cooled down to something well below its current thermonuclear state.

"Well, true. But obviously she expects us to be hot and heavy, right? I mean, this is the kind of stuff a woman wears for a man who can't keep his hands off her." Suddenly, she swept him with a glance that held a glittery sort of challenge. "We should probably practice that, don't you think?"

"What?" he squawked. "You want me to practice not being able to keep my hands off you?"

Actually, he needed to practice self-control, not the other way around. Restraint was the name of the game. Perfect. He could focus on that instead of the fact that the lingerie had been a gift, not a carefully crafted plan to drive him over the brink.

It was a testament to how messed up he was that he couldn't squelch his disappointment.

She nodded. "My sister just got married not too long ago and she's pretty open with me about how hot the sex is. I think she envisions all newlyweds being like that."

"That doesn't mean she expects us to strip down in your parents' foyer," he countered a little too forcefully. Mostly because he was envisioning how hot *this* newlywed couple could be. They could give Grace and her husband a run for her money, all right.

No. No, they could not.

Viv was not wearing the yellow lacy gateway to heaven for him tonight or any night. She wasn't challenging him to out-sex her sister's marriage. There was no sex at all in their future because Viv had a career she cared about and really didn't have time for a man's inconvenient attraction. Even if the man was her husband. Especially if the man was her husband who had promised to keep things platonic.

Of course he'd done that largely for himself. He'd never experienced such a strong physical pull before and he wasn't giving in to it no matter how badly he wanted to. There was a slippery edge between keeping himself out of trouble so he could honor his promise to his late friend and maintaining his integrity with Viv and his family about the nature of his marriage.

On that note, he needed to change the subject really fast. And get his rampant need under control before he lost everything.

Viv couldn't quite catch her breath. Her lungs ached to expand but the towel was in a precarious spot. If she breathed any deeper, it would slip completely from her nerveless fingers.

Though based on how long it was taking Jonas to clue in that this was a seduction scene, maybe throwing her boobs in his face would get the point across.

God, she sucked at this. Obviously. The girls on TV made it look so simple. She'd bet a million dollars that if this scene had happened on *Scandal*, the seductress would already be in the middle of her third orgasm.

Maybe she *should* have opened the wedding gift with Jonas instead of laying it out so he could find it. For some reason, she'd thought it would give him ideas. That he'd maybe take the lead and they could get something going while they had the perfect setup to indulge in the sparks that only burned hotter the longer they didn't consummate their marriage.

How was she supposed to prove she could be the opposite of clingy with a man she wanted more than oxygen if he wouldn't take her up on the invitation she'd been dangling in his face?

"Instead of practicing anything physical," Jonas said, "we should get our stories straight. We're not going to be hanging out with your family anytime soon but mine is just on the other side of the door. I don't want any missteps like the one at dinner where we didn't plan our responses ahead of time and somehow ended up promising to go to Korea."

"I don't mind going to Korea, Jonas. I would love to see it."

He shook his head with bemusement. "It's a sixteen-hour trip and that's only if there's a not a horribly long line in customs, which even a Kim cannot cut through. Trust me, I'm doing you a favor by not taking you."

How had they shifted from talking about hot sex to visiting his grandfather? That was not how this was supposed to go.

"Well, we have plenty of time to talk about our stories, too," she said brightly. "And the good news is that my hair is almost dry so the bathroom is yours. I like to read before going to sleep so I'll just be here whenever you're ready."

"Oh. Um…" Jonas glanced at the bed and back at her. "Okay. I was thinking about sleeping on the couch and setting an alarm—"

"You can't do that," she cut him off in a rush. That would ruin everything. "What if someone gets up for a midnight snack? Also, the couch would be so uncomfortable. Sleep here. I insist."

She shooed him toward the bathroom and the moment he shut the door, she dragged air into her lungs in deep gulps as she dropped the towel and twisted her hair into a modified updo at her crown, spilling tendrils down her cheeks. Then she slithered into the shameless yellow teddy and panties set that she'd picked out with Grace yesterday. Strictly so she could rub it in that she had a hot husband to wear it for, of course. And then she'd had Grace gift wrap it. The sly wink had been all her sister's idea, so she really hadn't fibbed much when she'd related the story to Jonas.

The lace chafed at her bare nipples, sending ripples of heat through her core. The panties rode high and tight, the strings threading between her cheeks.

Not a place she was used to having pressure and friction, but it was oddly exciting.

No wonder women wore this stuff. She felt sexy and more than a little turned on just by virtue of getting dressed. Who knew?

The sound of running water drifted through the walls as Jonas went through his nightly routine. She dove into bed and pulled up the covers until they were tight around her shoulders. Wait. That wasn't going to work. Experimentally, she draped the sheet across her chest like a toga, and threw her shoulders back. Huh. The one breast looked spectacular in the low-cut lace teddy, but the other one was covered up, which didn't seem like the point. Inching the sheet down, she settled into place against the pillow until she was happy with how she looked.

That was a lot of skin on *display*. Much more than she was used to. The lace left little to the imagination.

Surely this would be enough to entice Jonas into making the most of this opportunity to share a bedroom.

Light. She leaped up and slammed down the switch, leaving only the bedside lamp illuminated and leaped back under the covers. The doorknob to the bathroom rattled and she lost her nerve, yanking the sheet back up to cover the yellow lace until X-ray vision would be the only way Jonas could tell what she was wearing. He strode into the room.

Oh, God. Was a more delicious man ever created

in the history of time? He'd untucked his button-down and the tail hung casually below his waist. Plenty of access for a woman to slide her hands underneath. There was a gaping hole where his tie had been. A V framed a slice of his chest and he'd rolled his sleeves up to midforearm. It was the most undressed she'd ever seen him and her pulse quickened the closer he came.

This gorgeous creature was about to strip all that off and *get into bed*. With her. This was such a bad idea. Alluring and aloof was not in her wheelhouse and at that moment, she wanted Jonas with a full body ache that felt completely foreign and completely right at the same time.

"I thought you were going to be reading," he said, and stopped in the middle of the room as if he'd hit an invisible wall.

So close. And yet so far.

She shook her head, scrambling for a plausible excuse when she'd just said that was what she planned to do. Couldn't hold an e-reader and pretend you weren't wearing sexy lingerie that screamed *put your hands on me* at the same time.

In retrospect, that might have been a nice scene. She could have been reading with the tablet propped up on her stomach, which would have left her torso completely bare without making it look like she'd set up the scene that way. Dang it. Too late now.

"I couldn't find anything that held my attention."

"Oh. Okay."

And then the entire world fell away along with most of her senses as Jonas started unbuttoning his shirt. It was a slow, torturous event as he slipped the buttons free and each one revealed more of his beautiful body.

Thank God she hadn't stuck a book in front of her face. Otherwise she'd have missed the Jonas Striptease.

She glanced up to see his dark eyes on hers. Their gazes connected and she had the distinct impression he hadn't expected her to be watching him undress. But he didn't seem terribly unhappy about the audience, since he kept going. She didn't look away either.

He let the shirt fall, revealing first one shoulder, then the other. It shouldn't have been such a shock to see the indentations of muscles in his biceps as his arms worked off the shirt. She knew he hit the gym on a regular basis. They'd been friends for a year and talked about all manner of subjects. Sometimes he told her about his workout routine or mentioned that he'd switched it up and his arms were sore. Little had she realized what a visual panorama had been in store for her as a result.

"I feel like I should be wearing something sparkly underneath my pants," Jonas said with wry amusement. "Would it be possible for you to not watch me?"

"Oh. Um…sure." Cheeks on fire, she flipped over and faced the wall, careful to keep the sheet up around her neck. With the motion, it stretched tight. More mummy than Marilyn Monroe, but this was her first seduction. Surely even a woman like Marilyn had a few practice runs before she got it right. This one was Viv's.

And she needed a lot of practice, clearly, since she'd been caught staring and made Jonas uncomfortable at the same time. The whisper of fabric hitting the carpet made her doubly sorry she hadn't been facedown in a book when he came out of the bathroom because she could easily have pretended to be reading while watching the slow reveal out of the corner of her eye.

The bed creaked and the mattress shifted with Jonas's weight. "Still think this is a good idea?"

"I never said it was a good idea," she shot back over her shoulder. "I said our friendship could take it."

Which wasn't a given now that he was so close and so male and so much the subject of her fantasies that started and ended in a bed very much like this one. And she'd been forced to miss half of it due to Jonas's inconvenient sense of propriety. Well, he was done undressing now, right? This was her seduction and she wanted to face him. Except just as she rolled, he snapped off the bedside lamp, plunging the room into darkness.

"Good night," Jonas said, his voice sinfully rich in the dark.

The covers pulled a little as he turned over and settled into position. To go to sleep.

As mood killers went, that was a big one. She'd totally botched this.

Okay. Not totally. This was just a minor setback, most likely because she was trying to play hard to get, which was not as easy as it sounded, and frankly, not her typical method of operation. Plus? This was not a typical relationship. Jonas needed to keep her around, so by default this wasn't going to go like it had with her ex-boyfriends.

She had to approach this like a new recipe that hadn't quite turned out because she'd gone against her instincts and added an ingredient that she didn't like. And if she didn't like it, what was the point?

This was her cupcake to bake. Being the opposite of clingy and needy had only gotten her a disinterested husband—and rightfully so. How was he even supposed to know she wished he'd roll back over and explore the lingerie-clad body she'd hidden under the covers like a blushing virgin bride? Viv wasn't the kind of woman to inspire a man to slavish passion or it would have happened already.

She had to be smart if she couldn't be a femme fatale.

She blinked against the dark and tried not to focus on how the sound of Jonas breathing fluttered against her skin in a very distracting way. Somehow she was going to have to announce her interest in taking things to the next level in big bold letters without also giving him the impression she couldn't live without him. Though perhaps that last part wouldn't be too difficult; after all, she'd already been pretending for a year.

Six

After the weekend of torture, Jonas went to work on Monday with renewed determination to get his grandfather moving on the Park Industries merger. The sooner the ink was dry on that deal, the better. Then Jonas could get over his irritation that his marriage to Viv was what had tipped the scales toward his grandfather's decision to retire.

Grandfather recognized Jonas's accomplishments with Kim Electronics. Deep down, he knew that. But it rankled that the conversation about naming Jonas as the next CEO had come about *after* Grandfather had met Viv.

Didn't matter. The subject had come up. That was enough. And Jonas intended to make sure the subject didn't get dropped, because if he was forced to stay married to Viv, he should get something out of it. An Academy Award wouldn't be out of line after the stellar performance he'd turned in at his parents' house. How he'd acted like he'd been sleeping all night while lying next to his wife was still a mystery to him and he was the one who'd pulled it off.

Her scent still haunted him at odd moments. Like now. This conference call he'd supposedly been participating in had gotten maybe a quarter of his attention. Which was not a good way to prove he deserved the position of CEO.

But it was a perfect way to indulge in the memory of the sweet way she'd curled up next to him, her even breathing oddly arousing and lulling at the same time. He'd expected it to be weird the next morning, like maybe they wouldn't look each other in the eye, but Viv had awoken refreshed and beautiful, as if she'd gotten a great night's sleep. He pretended the same and they settled into an easy camaraderie around his parents that hadn't raised a single brow.

At least that part was over. Viv's mom and dad had invited them for dinner on Friday and he was plenty nervous about that experience. It would probably be fine. As long as he didn't have to act like he couldn't keep his hands off Viv. Or act like he didn't want to touch her. Actually, he'd lost track of *what* he was supposed to be doing. Hence the reason he hated lying. The truth was so much easier.

But when he got home that evening after a long

day that had included a two-hour debrief with Legal regarding the merger proposal, Viv was sitting on the couch with two glasses of wine. She smiled at him and he felt entirely incapable of faking anything. Especially if it came down to pretending he didn't want to be with her.

His answering smile broadened hers and that set off all sorts of fireworks inside that should have been a big fat warning to back off, but he was tired and there was absolutely nothing wrong with having a glass of wine with his friend Viv after work. That was his story and he was sticking to it.

"Are we celebrating something?" he asked as he hung his work bag on the hook near the refrigerator.

"Yes, that I can in fact open a bottle of wine all by myself." She laughed with that little peal he'd never noticed before he'd married her, but seemed to be a common occurrence lately. Or had she always laughed like that and he'd been too stuck in his own head to notice how warm it was?

"Was that in question?" He took the long-stemmed glass from her outstretched fingers and eased onto the couch next to her. Instantly, that turned into a big mistake as her scent wrapped around him. It slammed through his gut and his arm jerked, nearly spilling the wine.

For God's sake. This ridiculousness had to stop, especially before Friday or the second family trial by fire would end in a blaze.

"I'm just not talented in the cork-pulling arena,"

she answered casually as if she hadn't noticed his idiocy. "My skills start and end with baking."

Yes. Baking. They could talk about cupcakes while he got back on track. "Speaking of which, I wasn't expecting you home. Doesn't the shop stay open until seven on Mondays?"

She smiled. "You've been memorizing my work schedule? That's sweet. Josie is closing up for me. I wanted to be here when you got home."

"You did? Why?"

Because I couldn't stay away, Jonas. You're so much more interesting to me than cupcakes, Jonas. I want to strip you naked and have my wicked way with you, Jonas.

There came her gorgeous laugh again. He couldn't hear it enough, especially when he was in the middle of being such a doofus. If she was laughing, that was a good thing. Otherwise, he'd owe her an apology. Not that she could read his thoughts, thank God.

"I wanted to see you. We're still friends, right?"

Oh, yeah. "Right."

"Also, I wasn't kidding when I said my sisters are going to have an eagle eye on our relationship this Friday." Viv sipped her wine, her gaze on his over the rim. "We're still a little jumpy around each other. I'm not sure why, but sharing a bed didn't seem to help."

Huge mystery there. Maybe because his awareness level had shot up into the stratosphere since he'd woken up with a woman whom he hadn't touched one single time. Or it could be because he'd been kicking himself over his regret ever since. He shouldn't regret not touching her. It was the right move.

"No, it didn't help," he muttered. "That wasn't ever going to be the result of sleeping together platonically."

She nodded sagely. "Yes, I realized that sometime between then and now. Don't worry. I have a new plan."

"I wasn't worried. What is it?"

"We're trying too hard. We need to dial it back and spend time as friends. We were comfortable around each other then. It can totally be that way again."

That sounded really great to him. And also like there was a catch he couldn't quite see. Cautiously he eyed her. "What, like I take you to lunch and we just talk about stuff?"

"Sure." She shrugged and reached out to lace her fingers through his free hand. "See, we can hold hands and it doesn't mean anything. I'm just hanging out with my friend Jonas, whom I like. Hey, Jonas, guess what?"

He had to grin. This was not the worst plan he'd ever heard. In fact, it was pretty great. He'd missed their easy camaraderie and the lack of pretension. Never had she made him feel like he should be anything other than himself when they hung out. "Hey, Viv. What?"

"I made reservations at this new restaurant in Cary that sounds fab. It's Thai."

"That's my favorite." Which she well knew. It was hers, too. He took the first deep breath in what seemed like hours. They were friends. He could dang well act like one and stop nosing around Viv like a hormonal teenager.

"Drink your wine and then we'll go. My treat."

"No way. You opened the bottle of wine. The least I can do is spring for dinner."

"Well, it was a major accomplishment," she allowed, and clinked her glass to his as he held out the stemware. "I'm thrilled to have it recognized as such."

And the evening only got better from there. Jonas drove Viv to the restaurant and they chattered all the way about everything and nothing, which he'd have called a major accomplishment, too, since he managed to concentrate on the conversation and not on the expanse of Viv's bare leg mere inches from his hand resting on the gearshift. The food was good and the service exceptional.

As they walked in the door of the condo later, Jonas paused and helped Viv take off her jacket, then turned to hang it up for her in the foyer coat closet.

"I have to say," he called over his shoulder as he slid the hanger into place. "Dinner was a great idea."

He shut the door and Viv was still standing there in the foyer with a small smile.

"It's the best date I've been on in a long time," she said. "And seems like the plan worked. Neither of us is acting weird or jumpy."

"True." He'd relaxed a while back and didn't miss the edginess that had plagued him since the wedding ceremony. He and Viv were friends and that was never going to change. That was the whole reason he'd come up with this idea in the first place. "We may not set off the fire alarms when we visit with your family on Friday, but we can certainly pull off the fact that we like each other, which is not something all married couples can say."

That was fine with him. Better that way anyway. His reaction to the pull between him and Viv was ridiculous. So unlike him. He had little experience with something so strong that it dug under his skin, and he'd handled it badly.

Fortunately, he hadn't done anything irreversible that would have ruined their friendship. Though there'd been more than a handful of moments in that bed at his parents' that he'd been really afraid it was going to go the other way.

But then she stepped a little closer to him in the foyer, waltzing into his space without hesitation. The foyer was just a small area at the entrance of the condo with a coat closet and nothing more to recommend it. So there was little else to take his attention off the woman who'd suddenly filled it with her presence.

"We've been friends a long time," she said, and it was such a strange, unnecessary comment, but he nodded anyway because something had shifted in the atmosphere.

He couldn't put his finger on it. The relaxed, easy vibe from the restaurant had morphed into something else—a quickened sense of anticipation that he couldn't explain, but didn't hate. As if this really was a date and they'd moved on to the second part of the evening's activities.

"We've done a lot of firsts in the last little while," she continued, also unnecessarily because he was well aware that he'd shifted the dynamic of their relationship by marrying her.

"Yeah. Tonight went a long way toward getting us back to normal. To being friends without all the weirdness that sprang up when I kissed you."

That was probably the dumbest thing he could have said. He'd thrown that down between them and it was like opening the electrical panel of a television, where all the live components were exposed, and all it would take was one wrong move to fry the delicate circuitry.

Better to keep the thing covered.

But it was too late. Her gaze landed square on his mouth as if she was reliving the kiss, too. Not the nice and unexpectedly sweet kiss at the wedding ceremony. But the hot, tongue-on-tongue kiss outside her bedroom when they'd been practicing being a couple. The necessity of that practice had waned since his family had bought the marriage hook, line and sinker. Sure, they still had to get through her family, but he wasn't worried about it, racy lingerie gifts aside.

Now the only reason to ever kiss Viv again would be because he couldn't stop himself.

Which was the worst reason he could think of. And keep thinking about, over and over again.

"I don't think it was weirdness, Jonas," she murmured.

Instantly, he wished there was still some circumstance that required her to call him Mr. Kim. Why that was such a turn-on remained a mystery to him. But really, everything about Viv was a turn-on. Her laugh. Her cupcakes. The way her hair lay so shiny and soft against her shoulders.

"Trust me, it was weird," he muttered. "I gave myself entirely too many inappropriate thoughts with that kiss."

And that was the danger of being lulled back into a false sense of security with the sociable, uneventful dinner. He'd fallen into friendship mode, where he could say anything on his mind without consequence.

The admission that had just come out of his mouth was going to have consequences.

Her smile went from zero to sixty in less than a second and all at once, he wasn't sure the consequences were going to be anything close to what he'd envisioned. She waltzed even closer and reached up to adjust his tie in a provocative move that shouldn't have been as affecting as it was.

The tie hadn't needed adjusting. The knot was precisely where he'd placed it hours ago when he'd gotten dressed for work. It slid down a few centimeters and then a few more as she loosened it.

Loosened it. As if she intended to take it off.

But she stopped short of committing, which was good. Really…good. He swallowed as she speared him with her contemplative gaze, her hands still at his collar in an intimate touch. She was so close he could pull her into his arms if he wanted to.

He wanted to. Always.

Dinner hadn't changed that.

"The thing is, Jonas," she said. "I've had some thoughts, too. And if yours are the same as mine, I'm trying to figure out why they're inappropriate."

She flattened her hands on his lapels. The pressure sang through him and it would feel even better if he didn't have a whole suit jacket and two shirts between her palms and his skin.

The direction of this conversation floored him. And if she kept it up, the floor was exactly where they were going to end up.

"What are you saying, Viv?" he asked hoarsely, scrambling to understand. "That you lie awake at night and think about that kiss, aching to do it again?"

She nodded and something so powerful swept through his body that he could hardly breathe. This was the opposite of what should be happening. She should be backing off and citing her inability to focus on a man and her career at the same time. She was too busy, too involved in her business to date. This was the absolute he'd banked on for long agonizing hours, the thing that was keeping him from indulging in the forbidden draw between them.

Because if he gave in, he'd have no control over what happened next. That certainty had already been proven with what little they'd experimented so far. More would be catastrophic.

And so, so fantastically amazing.

"After tonight, I'm convinced we're missing an opportunity here," she said, her voice dripping with something sensual that he'd never have expected from his sunny friend Viviana Dawson. *Kim.*

Viv wasn't his friend. She was his wife. He'd been ignoring that fact for an entire day, but it roared back to the forefront with an implication he couldn't ignore. Except he didn't know what it meant to him, not really. Not just a means to an end, though it was an inescapable fact that she'd married him as a favor.

And he wanted to exploit that favor to get her naked and under him? It was improper, ridiculous. So very illicit that his body tightened with thick anticipation.

"What opportunity is that?" he murmured, letting his gaze flick over her face, searching for some sign that the answer about to come out of her mouth *was not* a green light to get naked.

Because he'd have a very difficult time saying no. In fact, he couldn't quite remember why he should say no. He shouldn't say no. If nothing else, taking this next step meant he wasn't lying to anyone about their marriage.

Her limpid brown eyes locked on to his. "We're both too busy to date. And even if we weren't, I have a feeling that 'oh, by the way, I'm married' isn't a great pickup line. You said it yourself. We spark. If our friendship can take a kiss, maybe it can take more. We should find out."

More. He liked the word *more* a lot. Especially if her dictionary defined it as lots and lots of sex while maintaining their friendship. If things got too intense, he could back off with no harm, no foul. It was like the absolute best of all worlds.

Unless that wasn't what she meant.

Clarification would be in order, just to be sure they were speaking the same language. "More?"

"Come on, Jonas." She laughed a little breathlessly and it trilled through him. "Are you going to make me spell it out?"

"Yes, I absolutely am," he growled, because the whole concept of Viv talking dirty to him was doing things to his insides that he was enjoying the hell out of. If he'd known dinner was *this* kind of date, he'd have skipped dessert. "I want to be crystal clear about what's on the table here."

Instead of suggesting things Jonas could do to her—all of which he'd immediately commit to memory so he didn't miss a single one—she watched him as she hooked the neckline of her dress and pulled it to the side. A flash of yellow seared his vision as his entire body tensed in recognition.

"I'm wearing my sister's gift," she murmured, and that admission was as much of a turn-on as any dirty talk. Maybe more so because he'd been fantasizing about that scrap of yellow lace for a million years.

"I bet it looks amazing on you."

"Only one way to find out," she shot back and curled her fingers around his lapels to yank him forward.

He met her mouth in a searing kiss without hesitation. All of his reservations melted in an instant as he sank into her, shaping her lips with his as he consumed her heat, letting it spread deep inside.

Why had he resisted this? Viv didn't want anything from him, didn't expect an emotional outpouring or even anything permanent. This was all going to end at some point and thus didn't count. No chance for romantic nonsense. No declarations of love would ever be forthcoming—on either side. Jonas's sense of honor would be intact, as would his sworn vow to Warren and Hendrix.

Instead of two friends pretending to be a married couple having sex, they were going to be married friends who *were* having sex. Living the truth appealed to him enormously. Desire swept through him as he got great handfuls of Viv's skin under his palms and everything but his wife drained from his mind.

* * *

Viv would have sworn on a truckload of Bibles that the kiss outside her bedroom last week had been the hottest one she'd ever participate in.

She'd have been wrong.

That kiss had been startling in its perfection. Unexpected in its heat. It had gotten her motor humming pretty fast. She'd been angling for another one just like that. Thank God she hadn't gotten her wish.

This kiss exploded in her core like a cannon. Desire crackled through the air as Jonas backed her up against the wall, crowding her against it with his hard body, demanding that her every curve conform to him. Her flesh rapidly obeyed. She nearly wept with the glory of Jonas pressed against her exactly as she'd fantasized hundreds of times.

He angled her jaw with his strong fingers until he got her situated the way he apparently wanted and then plunged in with the wickedest of caresses. His tongue slicked across hers so sensuously that she moaned against it, would have sagged if he hadn't had her pinned to the wall.

His hands nipped at her waist, skimmed upward and hooked both sides of the neckline. The fabric tore at the seams as he separated it from her shoulders, and she gasped.

"I need to see you," he murmured fiercely. "I'll buy you two to make up for this one."

And with that, the dress came apart in his hands. He peeled it from between them, following the line of the reveal with his hot mouth, laving at her exposed flesh until he caught the silk strap of the yellow teddy in his teeth, scraping the sensitive hollow of her shoulder.

The sensation shot through her center with tight, heated pulls. *Oh, my.* His fingers tangled in the strap, binding his palm to her shoulder as he explored the skin beneath the yellow lace with his tongue, dipping and diving into the holes of the pattern. Then his lips closed around her nipple through the fabric and her whole body jerked. Hot, wet heat dampened the scrap between her legs. The awareness that Jonas had drenched her panties so quickly only excited her more.

What had happened to the kind, generous man she'd been so intent on seducing? He'd become a hungry, untamed creature who wanted to devour her. She loved every second. His tongue flicked out to tease her nipple, wetting the lace, and it was wickedly effective. Moans poured from her throat as her head thunked back against the wall.

All at once, he sank to his knees and trailed his lips across the gap between the top and the bottom of her sexy lingerie set, murmuring her full name. *Viviana.* The sound of it rang in her ears as he worshipped her stomach with his mouth, and it was poetry.

Her thighs pressed together, seeking relief from the ache his touch had created, and she arched into his lips, his hands, crying out as his fingers worked under the hem of her soaked panties. The gorgeous man she'd married glanced up at her from his supine position, his gaze so wickedly hot that she experienced a small quake at that alone, but then he slid one finger along her crease, teasing her core until she opened wider, begging him to fill her.

He did. Oh, how he did, one quick motion, then back out again. The exquisite friction burned through her core a second time and she cried out.

"Please, Jonas" dripped from her mouth with little gasping sighs and she whimpered as she pleaded with him for whatever he planned to give her next.

She didn't know she could be this wanton, that the man she'd married could drive her to neediness so easily. It was so hot that she felt the gathering of her release before she was ready for the exquisite torture to end. No way to hold back. She crested the peak and came with hard ripples against Jonas's fingers. The orgasm drained her of everything but him.

Falling apart at his hands was better than what she'd dreamed of, hoped for, imagined—and then some. And it still wasn't over.

He nipped at her lace-covered sex and swept her up in his arms, still quaking, to carry her to his bedroom. Blindly, she tried to clear her senses long enough to gain some semblance of control. Why, she wasn't sure, but being wound up in Jonas's arms wearing nothing but wet lace while he was still fully dressed felt a lot like she'd surrendered more than she'd intended to.

But he wasn't finished with the revelations.

He laid her out on the comforter and watched her as he stripped out of his suit jacket and tie. She shivered long and hard as he began unbuttoning his shirt, but she didn't dare blink for fear of missing the greatest show on earth—the sight of her husband shedding his clothes. For her. Because she'd finally gotten him to see reason.

They were friends. What better foundation was there to get naked with someone than because you liked each other? It was sheer brilliance, if she did say so herself. The fact that she'd been racking her brain over how to best get to this place when the answer had been staring her in the face for a year? She'd rather not dwell on that.

Good thing she had plenty else to occupy her mind. That beautiful torso of his came into sight, still covered by a white undershirt that clung to his biceps and lean waist, and she wanted to touch him so badly her fingers tingled. But then his hands moved to his belt and she didn't move. Couldn't. Her lungs rattled with the need to expand. Slowly, the belt loosened and he pulled it from the loops. After an eternity, it dropped to the floor, followed shortly by the pants, and then came the pièce de résistance. Jonas stripped off his undershirt and worked off his boxers in the most spectacular reveal of all. Better than Christmas, her birthday and flipping the sign in Cupcaked's window to Open for the first time.

Her husband's body was gorgeous, long, lean. Vibrating with need that hungrily sniffed out hers as he crawled onto the bed and onto her, easily knocking her back to the mattress, covering her body with his.

And then she wasn't so coherent after that. His arms encircled her as easily as his dominant presence did. His kiss claimed her lips irrevocably, imprinting them with his particular brand of possession, the likes of which she'd never known. Never understood could exist.

The sensuous haze he dropped her into was delicious and she soaked it in, content to let him take his time as he explored her body with his hands more thoroughly than she'd have imagined possible when she still wore the yellow lace. She was so lost in him that it took her a minute to remember that she could indulge herself, too, if she wished.

Viv flattened her palms to his chest, memorizing the peaks and valleys of his body, reveling in the heat under her fingertips. She slid downward to cup his buttocks, shifting to align their hips because the ache at her core had only been awakened, not sated, and he had precisely what she needed.

He groaned deep in his throat as she circled against his thick, gorgeous erection, grinding her hips for maximum impact. The answering tilt of his hips enflamed her. As did the quickening of his breath.

"I need to be inside you," he murmured. "Before I lose my mind."

Rolling with her in his arms, he reached one hand

out to sling open the bedside table and extracted a box of condoms with ruthless precision. In seconds, he'd sheathed himself and rolled back into place against her.

His thumb slid into the indentation in her chin, levering her head up to lock his hot-eyed gaze onto her as he notched himself at her entrance.

The tip of his shaft tormented her, sensitizing everything it touched as he paused in the worst sort of tease.

"Jonas," she gasped.

"Right here, sweetheart. Tell me what you want."

"Everything." And she couldn't take it back, no matter how much of a mistake it was to admit that she wasn't the kind of woman who could be in the midst of such passion and hold back.

Except she wasn't entirely sure he meant for her to as he gripped her hip with his strong fingers, lifted and pushed in with a groan, spreading her wide as he filled her. The luscious solid length of him stretched her tight, and before she could question it, one tear slipped from the corner of her eye. It was a testament to the perfection of how he felt moving inside her, how wholly encompassing the sensations were that washed over her as Jonas made love to her.

And she was ten kinds of a fool if she thought she could keep pretending this was practice for her next relationship.

"Amazing. Beautiful. Mine." Words rained down on her from Jonas's mouth as he increased the tempo.

"I can't believe how this feels…you're so wet, so silky. I can't stop. Can't hold back."

For a woman who had never incited much more than mild interest in a man, to be treated to this kind of evidence that she was more than he could take—it was everything. "Give it all to me."

Unbelievably, there *was* more and he gave it to her, driving her to a soaring crescendo that made her feel more alive than anything in her memory. No longer was this bed a proving ground to show she could be with a man and not pour all of herself into him. He demanded her participation, wrung every drop of her essence out of her body.

She gladly surrendered it. Jonas was it for her, the man she'd married, the man she'd wanted for so very long.

As they both roared toward a climax, she had half a second to capture his face in her palms and kiss him with all the passion she could muster before they both shattered. She swallowed his groan and took the shudders of his body, absorbing them into hers even as she rippled through her own release. Everything was so much bigger, stronger, crisper than she'd have ever imagined and his mouth under hers curved into a blissful smile that her soul echoed.

And as he nestled her into his arms for a few badly needed moments of recovery time, she bit her lip against the wash of emotions that threatened to spill out all over their friendship.

She'd told him their relationship could take this.

Now she had to stick to her promise. How in the world she was going to keep him from figuring out that she was in love with him?

Seven

For the second day in a row, Jonas struggled to maintain his composure at work. It was for an entirely different reason today than it had been yesterday. But still. His wife swirled at the center of it and he wasn't sure what to do with that.

Last night had been legendary. Off the charts. Far more explosive than he would have ever guessed— and he'd spent a lot of time contemplating exactly how hot things with Viv could be.

She'd surpassed everything he'd ever experienced. Even here in his somewhat sterile office that had all the hallmarks of a CEO who ran a billion-dollar global company, his loins tightened the second he let his thoughts stray. She'd made him thoroughly question what he knew about how it could be between a man and a woman. How it could be between Jonas and Viv, more importantly, because he had a feeling they weren't done.

How could they be done? He'd barely peeled back the first layer of possibilities, and he was nothing if not ravenous to get started on the second and third layers. Hot Viv. Sensual Viv. The list could be endless.

Instead of drooling like an idiot over the woman he'd married, Jonas squared his shoulders and pushed the erotic images from his mind. The merger with Park was still just a nebulous concept and no one had signed anything. This was the deal of the century, and Jonas had to get it done before anyone thought twice about marriage alliances. Sun Park's grandfather could still pull the plug if he'd had his heart set on a much more intimate merger. Thus far, Jonas had done little but meet with Legal on it.

Four hours later, he had sketched out a proposed hierarchy for the business entities, worked through the human resources tangle of potential duplicate positions and then run the numbers on whether the Kim Building could support the influx of new people. His grandfather would be coming by soon to take a tour and this was exactly the data Jonas needed at his fingertips. Data that would solidify his place as the rightful CEO of Kim Electronics, with or without an *impulse of the heart* on his résumé.

So that was still a sore spot apparently. Jonas tried

to shrug it off and prepare for his grandfather's arrival, but wasn't at all surprised that Jung-Su showed up twenty minutes early. Probably a deliberate move to see if Jonas was prepared.

He was nothing if not ready, willing and able to prove that he was the right choice. He'd been preparing to be his grandfather's successor since college.

He strolled to the reception area, where his admin had made Grandfather comfortable. Technically Jung-Su was the boss of everyone in this building, but he hadn't visited America in several years. Jonas held the helm here and he appreciated that Grandfather didn't throw his weight around. They had professional, mutual respect for each other, which Jonas had to believe would ultimately hold sway.

Jung-Su glanced up as Jonas came forward, his weathered face breaking into a polite smile. Grandfather stood and they shook hands.

"Please follow me," Jonas said, and indicated the direction. "I'd like to show you the executive offices."

Jung-Su nodded and inclined his head, but instead of following Jonas, he drew abreast and walked in lockstep toward the elevator. Over the weekend, they'd done a lot of sitting down and Jonas hadn't noticed how much his grandfather had shrunk. Jonas had always been taller and more slender to his grandfather's stocky build, but more so now, and it was a visual cue that his grandfather had aged. As much as Jonas had focused on getting his grandfather comfortable with passing the mantel, he'd given little thought to the idea that becoming the next CEO of the global company meant his mentorship with Jung-Su would be over.

"Tell me," Grandfather said as they reached the elevator. "How is your lovely wife?"

"She's…" *A vixen in disguise.* Not the kind of information his grandfather was looking for with the innocuous question. "Great. Her shop is constantly busy."

And Viv had ducked out early to take him on the ride of his life last night. For the first time, he wondered if she'd planned the evening to end as it had or if it had been as spontaneous on her part as it had been on his. Maybe she'd been thinking about getting naked since the weekend of torture, too. If so, he liked that she'd been similarly affected.

They rode two floors up to the executive level. As they exited, Jonas and Jung-Su nodded to the various employees going about the business of electronics in a beehive of activity.

"You've mentioned your wife's business frequently," his grandfather commented just outside the boardroom where Jonas conducted the majority of his virtual meetings. "Doesn't she have other interests?"

The disapproval in his grandfather's voice was faint. "You don't understand. Her bakery is much more than just a business. It's an extension of her."

Cupcakes had been a mechanism to fit in among

her older, more accomplished sisters, as she'd told him on numerous occasions. But it had morphed from there into a business that she could be proud of. Hell, it was a venture *he* was proud of.

"Anyone can pull a package of cupcake mix off the shelf at the grocery store," Jonas continued, infusing as much sincerity into his speech as he could. His grandfather had no call to be throwing shade at his wife's profession. "That's easy. Viv spends hours in her kitchen doing something special to hers that customers can't get enough of."

"It seems as if you are smitten by her cupcakes, as well," Grandfather commented with a tinge of amusement.

Jonas forced a return smile that hopefully didn't look as pained as he suspected it did. *Smitten*. He wasn't smitten with Viv and it rankled that he'd managed to convince his grandfather that he was. Cupcakes, on the other hand—no pretending needed there. "Of course I am. That's what first drew me to her."

Like it was yesterday, he recalled how many times he'd found excuses to drop by Cupcaked to get a glimpse of Viv in those first few weeks after meeting her. Often she was in the back but if she saw him, she popped out for a quick hi, ready with a smile no matter what she had going on in the kitchen. That alone had kept him coming back. There was always someone in the office with a birthday or anniversary, and cupcakes always made an occasion more festive.

"Ah, yes, I recall that conversation at dinner where she mentioned you pretended to go there for her cupcakes but were really there to see her."

"It was both," he corrected easily since it was true. He could own that he liked Viv. They were friends.

Who'd seen each other naked.

Before he could stop it, images of Viv spilled through his mind.

The rush of heat to his body smacked him, sizzling across his skin so fast he had little chance of reeling it back. But he had to. This was the most inappropriate time to be thinking about his wife wearing that see-through yellow lacy concoction strictly for his benefit.

"Pardon me for a moment," Jonas croaked, and ducked into the executive washroom to get himself under control. Or as close to it as he could with an enormous erection that showed no signed of abating.

And while he stood in front of the mirror concentrating on his breathing and doing absolutely nothing constructive, he pulled out his phone to set a reminder to drop by the jewelry store on the way home. Viv had expressly asked for jewels as compensation for the favor she was doing him. She needed something pretty and ridiculously expensive.

Thinking of her draped in jewelry he'd bought wasn't helping.

After the longest five minutes of his life, Jonas finally got the tenting mostly under control. No one had noticed. Or at least that's what he tried to tell himself. His staff didn't walk around with their eyes on his crotch.

The biggest hit was to Jonas's psyche. How had he let Viv get under his skin like that? It was unacceptable. If nothing else, he needed to maintain his professionalism during this period when his grandfather's support meant everything. There were other contenders for Jung-Su's job, such as vice presidents who lived in Korea and had worked alongside the CEO for thirty years. Some of Mr. Park's staff could rise to the top as worthy heads of a global company, and those under the Park umbrella arguably had more experience running the factories that would come into play with the merger.

Jonas had to reel it back with Viv. Way back. There was no excuse for falling prey to baser urges and he definitely didn't want to find out what happened next if he kept going down this path. That was one absolute he trusted—the less he let a woman get tangled up in his emotions, the better.

Resolute, Jonas returned to find his grandfather in deep discussion with Jonas's chief financial officer, a man without whom Kim Electronics would suffer in the American market.

Perfect. This was an opportunity to guide the discussion to Jonas's accomplishments as well as those of his staff, who were a reflection of his ability to run the Americas branch. Back on track, Jonas smiled at the two men and jumped into the conversation as if he hadn't just had a minor freak-out over an incontrollable urge to drive straight home and bury himself in his wife.

That wasn't happening. Boundaries needed to happen. Jonas didn't have the luxury of letting his wife dig further under his skin. But when he got home later that night, it was to an empty house, and boundaries didn't seem like such a fun plan.

More disappointed than he had a right to be, Jonas prowled around the enormous condo to be sure Viv hadn't tucked herself away in a corner to read or watch TV. *Nada*. He glanced at his watch. It was well after seven. She must have gotten caught up at the shop. Totally her right to work late. They didn't answer to each other.

For a half second, he contemplated walking the four blocks to Cupcaked. Strictly so he could give Viv her gift, of course. But that smacked of eagerness to see her that he had no intention of admitting to. So instead, he flopped on the couch and scrolled through his never-ending inbox on his phone, desperate for something to take his mind off the resounding silence in the condo. Wow, was it quiet. Why had he never noticed that before? The high ceilings and exposed beams usually created an echo that reminded him of a museum, but he'd have to be making noise for that echo to happen.

Viv had made a lot of noise last night, but he hadn't been paying a whole lot of attention to whether the sounds of her gasps and sighs had filled the cavernous part of the loft. And now he was back to thinking about his wife, her gorgeous body and why she wasn't currently naked in his lap.

He scowled. They'd done zero to establish how their relationship would progress after last night. They should have. *He* should have. Probably the smartest thing would have been to establish that last night was a onetime thing. He couldn't keep having meltdowns at work or moon around over whether Viv planned to hang out with him at night.

He should find something else to do. Like... He glanced around the condo, suddenly at a loss. Prior to getting married, what had he done on a random Tuesday when he was bored?

Nothing. Because he was rarely bored. Usually he had work and other stuff to occupy him. *Friends.* Of course the answer was to ping his friends. But Warren didn't respond to his text message and Hendrix was in New York on a business trip.

Viv's key rattled in the lock. Finally. He vaulted off the couch to greet her, totally not okay with how his pulse quickened at the prospect of seeing her and completely unsure how to stop it.

As she came through the door, her smile widened as she spied Jonas standing in the hall, arms crossed, hip casually cocked out against the wall.

"Hi," she said, halting just short of invading his space. "Were you waiting for me?"

No sprang to his lips before he thought better of it. Well, he couldn't really deny that, now, could he? If he'd stayed sprawled on the couch and given her a casual "what's up?" as she strolled through the door, he might have had a leg to stand on. Too late.

"Yeah," he admitted, and held up the shiny blue foil bag clutched in his fingers. "I have something for you."

Her eyes widened as she held out her hand to accept the bag. The most delicious smell wafted between them, a vanilla and Viv combo that made him think of frosting and sex and about a million other things that shouldn't go together but did—like marriage and friendship.

Why couldn't he greet his wife at the door if he felt like it? It wasn't a crime. It didn't mean anything.

The anticipation that graced her smile shouldn't have pleased him so much. But he couldn't deny that it whacked him inside in a wholly different way than the sultry smile she'd laid on him last night, right before she informed him that she had on yellow lingerie under her clothes.

Which was not up for a repeat tonight. Boundaries should be the first order of business. Viv had sucked him down a rabbit hole that he didn't like. Well, he *liked* it. It just didn't sit well with how unbelievably tempting she was. If she could tempt him into letting go of his professionalism, what other barriers could she knock down? The risk was not worth it.

But then she opened the box, and her startled gasp put heat in places that he should be able to control a hell of lot better.

"Jonas, this is too much," she protested with a

laugh and held out the box like she expected him to take it back or something.

"Not hardly. It's exactly right." Before she got ideas in her head about refusing the gift that had taken him thirty minutes to pick out, he plucked the diamond necklace from its velvet housing and undid the clasp so he could draw it around her neck. "Hush, and turn around."

She did and that put him entirely too close to her sweet flesh. That curve where her shoulder flared out called to him. Except it was covered by her dress. That was a shame.

Dragging her hair out of the way, she waited for him to position the chain. He let the catch of the necklace go and the ten-carat diamond dropped to rest against her chest, just above the swell of her breasts. Which were also covered, but he knew precisely where they began.

His lips ached to taste that swell again. Among other things. Palms flat across her back, he smoothed the chain into place, but that was really just an excuse to touch her.

"If you're sure," she murmured, and she relaxed, letting her body sink backward until it met his and heat flared between them.

"Oh, I'm sure." She'd meant about the diamond. Probably. But his mouth had already hit the bare spot she'd revealed when she'd swept her long brown hair aside and the taste of Viv exploded under his tongue.

Groaning, he let his hands skim down her waist

until he found purchase and pulled until their bodies nested together tighter than spoons in a drawer. The soft flesh of her rear cradled the iron shaft in his pants, thickening his erection to the point of pain. He needed a repeat of last night. Now.

He licked the hollow of her collarbone, loving the texture under his tongue. More Viv needed. Her answering gasp encouraged him to keep going.

Gathering handfuls of her dress, he yanked it from between them and bunched it at her waist, pressing harder into the heat of her backside the moment he bared it. His clothes and a pair of thin panties lay between him and paradise, and he wanted all that extraneous fabric gone.

She arched against him as his fingers cruised along the hem of her drenched underwear and he took that as agreement, stripping them off in one motion. Then he nudged her legs wider, opening her sex, and indulged them both by running a fingertip down the length of her crease. Her hands flew out and smacked the wall and she used it to brace as she ground her pelvis into his.

Fire tore through his center and he needed to be inside her with an uncontrollable urge, but the condoms were clear across the cavernous living area in his bedside table. He couldn't wait. Viv cried out his name as he plunged one then two fingers into her center, groaning at the slick, damp heat that greeted him. She was so wet, so perfect.

As he fingered her, she shuddered, circling her

hips in a frenzied, friction-induced madness that pushed him to the brink. Her hot channel squeezed his fingers and that was nearly all she wrote. Did she have a clue how much he wanted to yank his zipper down, impale her and empty himself? Every muscle in his body fought him and his will crumbled away rapidly. Reaching between them, he eased open his belt.

But then she came apart in his arms, huffing out little noises that drove him insane as she climaxed. His own release roared to the forefront and all it would take was one tiny push to put him over the edge. Hell, he might not even need a push. Shutting his eyes against the strain, he drew out her release with long strokes that made her whimper.

She collapsed in his arms as she finished and he held her upright, murmuring nonsense to her as she caught her breath.

"Let me take you to bed," he said, and she nodded, but it was more of a nuzzle as she turned her cheek into his.

To hell with boundaries.

He hustled her to his room, shed his clothes and hers without ripping anything this time—because he was in control—and finally she was naked. Sultry smile in place, she crawled onto the bed and rolled into a provocative position that begged him to get between her legs immediately and hammer after his own release. But despite being positive the only thing he could possibly do next was get inside her as fast as humanly possible, he paused, struck immobile all at once.

That was *his wife* decked out on the bed.

The sight bled through him, warming up places inside dangerously fast. Places that weren't what he'd call normal erogenous zones. And that's when he realized his gaze was on her smile. Not her body.

What was wrong with him? A naked woman was on display for his viewing pleasure. He forced his gaze to her breasts, gratified when the pert tips pebbled under his watchfulness. That was more like it. This was about sex and how good two people could make each other feel.

With a growl, he knelt on the bed and kissed his way up her thigh. He could absolutely keep his hands off her if he wanted to. He had total control over his desires, his emotions. There was nothing this woman could do to drive him to the point of desperation, not in bed and certainly not out of it. To prove it, he pushed her thighs open and buried his face between them.

She parted for him easily, her throaty cry washing over him as he plunged his tongue into her slickness. That wet heat was *his*. He'd done that to her and he lapped at it, groaning as her musky scent flooded his senses. The ache in his groin intensified into something so strong it was otherworldly. He needed to feel her tight, slick walls close around him, to watch her face as it happened. He needed it, but denied himself because she didn't own his pleasure. He owned hers.

Her hips rolled and bucked. He shoved his mouth deeper into her center as she silently sought more, and he gave it to her. Over and over he worked his lips and tongue against her swollen flesh until she bowed up with a release that tensed her whole body. And then she collapsed against the mattress, spilling breathy, satisfied sighs all over him. Only then did he permit his own needs to surge to the surface.

Fingering on a condom that he'd retrieved from the drawer, he settled over her and indulged his intense desire to kiss her. She eagerly took his tongue, sucking it into her hot mouth, and he groaned as he transferred her own taste back to her. Their hips came together, legs tangling, and before he could fully register her intent, she gathered him up in her tight fist and guided him into the paradise at her core.

A strong urge to fill her swelled. But he held on by the scrabbly edge of his fingertips, refusing to slam into her as he ached to do. Slowly, so slowly that he nearly came apart, he pushed. Her slickness accepted him easily, wringing the most amazing bliss from a place he scarcely recognized. The deeper he sank, the better it felt.

Her gaze captured his and he fell into her depths. She filled him, not the other way around. How was that physically possible? He couldn't fathom it, but neither could he deny it. Or halt the rush of Viviana through his veins as she streamed straight to his heart in a kill shot that flooded all four chambers at once.

And then there was nothing but her and the unbelievable feel of her skin against his, her desire soaking through his pores in an overwhelming deluge. He meant to hold back, determined to prove something that escaped him as she changed the angle. Somehow that allowed him to go deeper, push harder. Her cries spurred him on, and unbelievably, she took it higher, sucking him under into a maelstrom of sensation and heightened pleasure.

When her hips began pistoning in countermeasure to his, it nearly tore him in two. Delirious with the need to come, he grabbed one of her legs and pushed at the knee, opening her wider so he had plenty of room to finger her at the source of her pleasure. Two circular strokes and she climaxed, squeezing him so tight that it tripped the wire on his own release.

Bright pinpoints of light streamed behind his eyes as he came so hard that he would have easily believed he'd crossed over into an alternate dimension. In this new dimension, he could let all the things crowding through his chest spill out of his mouth. But those things shouldn't exist in any universe.

If he didn't acknowledge them, they didn't exist. Then he wouldn't be breaking his word.

As his vision cleared and his muscles relaxed, rendering him boneless, he collapsed to the mattress, rolling Viv into his arms.

The heavy diamond swung down from the chain he'd latched around her neck, whacking him on the shoulder. He fingered it back into place silently, weighing out whether he could actually speak or if that spectacular orgasm had in fact stolen his voice.

"I get the sense you've been saving up," Viv commented huskily, her lips moving against his chest, where her face had landed after he'd nestled her close. Probably he shouldn't have done that, but he liked coming down from a post-lovemaking high with her in his arms.

"It's been a while," he allowed. "I mean, other than last night, obviously."

Her mouth curved up in a smile. "Both times were amazing. I could get used to this."

He could, too. That was enough to get the panic really rolling. "We should probably talk about that."

To soften the blow, he threaded some of her pretty, silky hair through his fingers. That felt so nice, he kept going, running all the way down her head to her neck and back again.

"Mmm," she purred, pressing into his fingers, which were somehow massaging her with little strokes that she clearly liked. "I'm listening."

"We're still friends, right?" Pathetic. That hadn't been what he'd intended to say at all, but now that it was out there…it was exactly what he wanted to know. He wanted to hear her say that having an amazing encounter that he'd felt to his soul hadn't really affected her all that much. Then he could keep lying to himself about it and have zero qualms.

"Sure."

She kissed his chest right above his nipple and

then flicked her tongue across the flat disk. Flames erupted under his skin, fanning outward to engulf his whole body, including his brain, because he suddenly couldn't recall what he'd been so convinced he needed to establish.

Then she slung a leg over his, nestling her thigh against the semi-erection that grew a lot less semi much faster than he would have credited, considering how empty he'd have sworn he was already.

"Geez, Viv." He bit back the curse word that had sprung to his lips. "You're insatiable."

Not that he was complaining. Though he should be saying something that sounded a lot like "Let's dial it back about one hundred and eighty degrees."

"You make me that way," she said throatily. "I've been celibate for like a billion years and that was totally okay, but all of a sudden, you kiss me and I can't think. I just want to be naked with you 24/7."

"Yeah?" he growled. That pretty much mirrored his thoughts perfectly. "That can be arranged."

No. No, it could not.

He had a merger to manage. Reins to pick up from his grandfather. What was he talking about, letting Viv coerce him into a day-and-night screw fest? That sounded like a recipe for disaster, especially given how strong his reactions to her were. They needed to cool it off.

"We can't." She sighed. "I've got a mountain of paperwork and Josie requested the rest of the week off so she can study for final exams. As nice as this is, we should probably back off for a while. Don't you think?"

"Absolutely not." Wrong answer. *Open your mouth and take it back.* "We're doing fine winging it. Aren't we? There's no pressure. If you come home from work hot and needy and want to strip down in the foyer to let me take care of you, I'm perfectly fine with that."

In fact, he'd gladly etch that date on his planner with a diamond drill bit. Mental note: buy Viv more jewelry and more racy lingerie. If he really tried, he could space out the gifts, one a night for oh, at least two weeks.

She arched a brow. "Really? This isn't feeling a little too real?"

His mood deflated. And now he was caught in a trap of his own making. He couldn't lie to Viv, but neither could he admit that it had been feeling too real since the ceremony. The same one he'd tried to sell to Warren and Hendrix as a fake wedding when Warren had clued in immediately that there was nothing fake about any of this.

This was what he got for not nodding his head the second the words *back off* came out of her mouth.

"See, the thing is," he began and would have sworn he'd been about to say that being friends with no benefits worked better for him. But that's not what happened. "I need this to be real. I don't have to pretend that I'm hot for you, because I am. We don't have to sell that we're burning up the sheets when we have dinner with your family on Friday. Why not keep going? The reasons we started this are still true. Unless I've dissatisfied you in some way?"

"Oh, God. No!" Her hand flew to her mouth. "Not in the slightest. You're the hottest lover I've ever had, bar none."

That pleased him enormously. "Then stop talking about easing off. We can be casual about it. Sometimes you sleep in my bed. Sometimes you don't. No rules. We're just friends who're having really great sex."

"That sounds like a plan."

She shrugged like she could take it or leave it, which raked across his spine with a sharpness that he didn't like. She obviously wasn't feeling any of the same things he was. She'd been a half second from calling it quits. Would have if he hadn't stopped her.

"Great." And somehow he'd managed to appease his sense of honor while agreeing to continue sleeping with his wife in what was shaping up to be the hottest affair he'd ever had.

It was madness. And he couldn't wipe the grin off his face.

Eight

If there was a way to quit Jonas, Viv didn't want to know about it.

She should be looking for the exit, not congratulating herself on the finest plea for remaining in a man's bed that had ever been created in the history of time. She couldn't help it. The scene after the most explosive sexual encounter of her life had been almost as epic. Jonas had no idea how much it had killed her to act so nonchalant about ending things. He'd been shocked she'd suggested backing off. It had been written all over his face.

That kept her feeling smug well into the dawn hours the next morning. She rolled toward the middle of the bed, hoping to get a few minutes of snuggle time before work. Cold sheets met her questing fingers. Blinking an eye open, she sought the man she'd gone to sleep with.

Empty. Jonas had gotten out of bed already. The condo was quiet. Even when she was in her bedroom, she could hear the shower running through the pipes in the ceiling—a treat she normally enjoyed, as she envisioned the man taking a shower in all his naked glory.

Today, she didn't get that luxury, as Jonas was clearly already gone. Profoundly disappointed that he hadn't kissed her goodbye, said goodbye or thought about her at all, she climbed out from under the sheets and gathered up her clothes for the return trek to her bedroom.

It was fine. They'd established last night that there were no rules. No pressure. When he'd gotten on board with convincing her that they could keep sleeping together—which she still couldn't quite believe she'd orchestrated so well—she'd thought that meant they were going to spend a lot of time together. Be goofy and flirty with each other. Grow closer and closer until he looked up one day and realized that friendship plus marriage plus sex equaled something wonderful, lasting and permanent. Obviously she'd thought wrong.

The whole point had been to give him the impression she wasn't clingy. That Independence was her middle name and she breezed through life just fine, thanks, whether she had a man or not. Apparently he'd bought it. *Go me.*

The sour taste wouldn't quite wash from her mouth no matter how much mouthwash she used. After a long shower to care for her well-used muscles, Viv wandered to the kitchen barefoot to fight with Jonas's espresso machine. She had a machine at Cupcaked but Jonas's was a futuristic prototype that he'd brought home from work to test. There were more buttons and gizmos than on a spaceship. Plus, it hated her. He'd used it a couple of times and made it seem so easy, but he had a natural affinity with things that plugged in, and the machine had his name on it, after all. Finally, she got a passably decent latte out of the monstrosity.

She stood at the granite countertop to drink it, staring at the small, discreet Kim Electronics logo in the lower right-hand corner of the espresso machine. Jonas's name had been emblazoned on her, too, and not just via the marriage license and subsequent trip to the DMV to get a new driver's license. He'd etched his name across her soul well before they'd started sleeping together. Maybe about the third or fourth time they'd had lunch.

Strange then that she could be so successful with snowing him about her feelings. It had never worked with any man before. Of course, she'd never tried so hard to be cool about it. Because it had never mattered so much.

But now she wasn't sure what her goal here really

was. Or what it should be. Jonas had "talked" her into keeping sex on the menu of their relationship. She'd convinced him their friendship could withstand it. Really, the path was pretty clear. They were married friends with benefits. If she didn't like that, too bad.

She didn't like it.

This wasn't practice for another relationship and neither was it fake, not for her. Which left her without a lot of options, since it was fake to Jonas.

Of course, she always had the choice to end things. But why in the world would she want to do that? Her husband was the most amazing lover on the planet, whose beautiful body she could not get enough of. He bought her diamonds and complimented her cupcakes. To top it all off, Viv was *married*. She'd been after that holy grail for ages and it had felt really nice to flash her ring at her sisters when they'd come to the shop last week. It was the best possible outcome of agreeing to do this favor for Jonas.

Convinced that she should be happy with that, she walked the four blocks to Cupcaked and buried herself in the kitchen, determined to find a new cupcake flavor to commemorate her marriage. That was how she'd always done things. When something eventful occurred, she baked. It was a way of celebrating in cake form, because wasn't that the whole point of cake? And then she had a cupcake flavor that reminded her of a wonderful event.

The watermelon recipe she'd been dying to try didn't turn out. The red food coloring was supposed to be tasteless but she couldn't help thinking that it had added something to the flavor that made the cupcake taste vaguely like oil. But without it, the batter wasn't the color of watermelon.

Frustrated, she trashed the whole batch and went in search of a different food coloring vendor. Fruitless. All her regular suppliers required an industrial sized order and she couldn't commit to a new brand without testing it first.

She ended up walking to the market and buying three different kinds off the shelf. For no reason, apparently, as all three new batches she made didn't turn out either. Maybe watermelon wasn't a good cupcake flavor. More to the point, maybe she shouldn't be commemorating a fake marriage that was real to her but still not going to last. That was the problem. She was trying to capture something fleeting that shouldn't be immortalized.

After the cupcake failure, her mood slid into the dumps. She threw her apron on the counter and stayed out of the kitchen until lunch, when she opened for business to the public. On the plus side, every display case had been cleaned and polished, and the plate-glass window between Cupcaked and the world had not one smudge on it. Camilla wouldn't be in until after school, so Viv was by herself for the lunch rush, which ended up being a blessing in disguise.

Wednesday wasn't normally a busy day, but the line stretched nearly out the door for over an hour.

Which was good. Kept her mind off the man she'd married. Josie had the rest of the week off, and Viv had approved it thinking she and Camilla could handle things, but if this kind of crowd was even close to a new normal, she might have to see about adding another part-time employee. That was a huge decision, but a good sign. If she couldn't have Jonas, she could have her cupcakes. Just like she'd always told him.

After locking the bakery's door, tired but happy with the day's profits, she headed home. On the way, she sternly lectured herself about her expectations. Jonas might be waiting in the hall for her to come in the door like he had been last night. Or he might not. Her stomach fluttered the entire four blocks regardless. Her husband had just been so sexy standing there against the wall with a hot expression on his face as if he planned to devour her whole before she completely shut the door.

And then he pretty much had, going down on her in the most erotic of encounters. She shuddered clear to her core as she recalled the feel of that first hot lick of his tongue.

Oh, who was she kidding? She couldn't stop hoping he'd be waiting for her again tonight. Her steps quickened as she let herself anticipate seeing Jonas in a few minutes.

But he wasn't in the hall. Or at home. That sucked.

Instead of moping, she fished out her phone and called Grace. It took ten minutes, but eventually her sister agreed to have dinner with Viv.

They met at an Italian place on Glenwood that had great outdoor seating that allowed for people watching. The maître d' showed them to a table and Grace gave Viv a whole three seconds before she folded her hands and rested her chin on them.

"Okay, spill," she instructed. "I wasn't expecting to see you before Friday. Is Jonas in the doghouse already?"

"What? No." Viv scowled. Why did something have to be wrong for her to ask her sister to dinner? Besides, that was none of Grace's business anyway. Viv pounced on the flash of green fire on her sister's wrist in a desperate subject change. "Ooooh, new bracelet? Let me see."

The distraction worked. Grace extended her arm dutifully, her smile widening as she twisted her wrist to let the emeralds twinkle in the outdoor lighting. "Alan gave it to me. It's an anniversary present."

"You got married in April," Viv said.

"Not a wedding anniversary. It's a...different kind of anniversary."

Judging by the dreamy smile that accompanied that admission, she meant the first time she and Alan had slept together, and clearly the act had been worthy of commemorating.

Viv could hardly hide her glee. It was going to be one of *those* discussions and she *finally* got to participate. "Turns out Jonas is big on memorializing spectacular sex, too."

"Well, don't hold back. Show and tell." Grace waggled her brows.

Because she wanted to and she could, Viv fished the diamond drop necklace from beneath her dress and let it hang from her fingers. Not to put too fine a point on it, but hers was a flawless white diamond in a simple, elegant setting. Extremely appropriate for the wife of a billionaire. And he'd put it around her neck and then given her the orgasm of her life.

The baubles she could do without and had only mentioned jewelry in the car on the way to Jonas's parents' house because he'd pushed her to name something he could do for her. She hadn't really been serious. But all at once, she loved that Jonas had unwittingly allowed her to stand shoulder to shoulder with her sister when it came to talking about whose marriage was hotter.

"Your husband is giving you jewelry already?" Grace asked, and her tone was colored with something that sounded a lot like she was impressed. "Things must be going awfully well."

"Oh, yeah, of course," Viv commented airily and waved her hand like she imagined a true lady of the manor would. "We didn't even make it out of the foyer where he gave it to me before his hands were all over me."

Shameless. This was the raciest conversation she'd ever had with anyone except maybe Jonas, but that didn't count. She should be blushing. Or something. Instead she was downright giddy.

"That's the best." Grace's dreamy smile curved back into place. "When you have a man who loves you so much that he can't wait. I'm thrilled you finally have that."

Yeah, not so much. Her mood crashed and burned as reality surfaced. Viv nodded with a frozen expression that she hoped passed for agreement.

Obviously Grace knew what it felt like to have a man dote on her and give her jewelry because he cared, not because they were faking a relationship. Grace could let all her feelings hang out as much as she wanted and Alan would eat it up. Because they were in love.

Something that felt a lot like jealousy reared its ugly head in the pit of Viv's stomach. Which was unfair and petty, but recognizing it as such didn't make it go away.

"Jonas was worth waiting for," she said truthfully, though it rankled that the statement was the best she could do. While Viv's husband might rival her sister's in the attentive lover department, when it came to matters of the heart, Grace and Alan had Viv and Jonas beat, hands down.

"I'm glad. You had a rough patch for a while. I started to worry that you weren't going to figure out how stop putting a man's emotional needs ahead of yours. It's good to see that you found a relationship that's on equal footing."

Somehow, Viv managed to keep the surprise off

her face, but how, she'd never know. "I never did that. What does that even mean?"

"Hon, you're so bad at putting yourself first." Grace waved the waiter over as he breezed by and waited until he refilled both their wineglasses before continuing. "You let everyone else dictate how the relationship is going to go. That last guy you dated? Mark? He wanted to keep things casual, see other people, and even though that's not what you wanted, you agreed. Why did you do that?"

Eyebrows hunched together, Viv gulped from her newly filled wineglass to wet her suddenly parched throat. "Because when I told him that I wanted to be exclusive, he said I was being too possessive. What was I supposed to do, demand that he give me what I want?"

"Uh, *yeah*." Grace clucked. "You should have told him to take a hike instead of waiting around for him to do it for you."

"It really didn't take that long," she muttered, but not very loud, because Grace was still off on her tangent.

Her sister was right. Viv should have broken up with Mark during that exact conversation. But on the heels of being told she was "clingy," "controlling" and "moving too fast" by Zachary, Gary and Judd respectively, she hadn't wanted to rock the boat.

Why was it such a big deal to want to spend time with a man she was dating? It wasn't clingy. Maybe it was the wine talking, but Grace's point wasn't lost on Viv—she shouldn't be practicing her independence but finding a different kind of man. One who couldn't stand being apart from her. One who texted her hearts and smiley faces just to let her know he was thinking of her. One who was in love with her.

In other words—not Jonas.

The thought pushed her mood way out of the realm of fit for company. Dinner with Grace was a mistake. Marrying Jonas had been a mistake. Viv had no idea what she was doing with her life or how she was going to survive a fake marriage she wished was real.

"I just remembered," she mumbled. "I have to… do a thing."

Pushing back from the table, Viv stood so fast that her head spun. She'd planned to walk home but maybe a cab would be a better idea.

"What?" Grace scowled. "You called me. I canceled drinks with the ladies from my auxiliary group. How could you forget that you had something else?"

Because Viv wasn't perfect like Grace with the perfect husband who loved her, and frankly, she was sick of not getting what she wanted. "Jonas has scrambled my wits."

Let her sister make what she would out of that. Viv apologized and exited the restaurant as quickly as she could before she started crying. After not seeing Jonas this morning and the watermelon-slash-red-food-coloring disaster and the incredibly busy day at the store and then realizing that she had not in fact gotten to join the club her sisters were in, crying was definitely imminent.

The icing on the cake happened when she got home and Jonas was sprawled on the couch watching TV, wearing jeans with a faded Duke T-shirt that clung to his torso like a second skin.

His smile as he glanced up at her was instant and brilliant and that was all it took to unleash the waterworks.

With tears streaming down her face, Viv stood in the foyer of the condo she shared with Jonas until whatever point in the future he decided to pull the plug on their marriage and it was all suddenly not okay.

"Hey, now. None of that." Jonas flicked off the TV and vaulted to his feet, crossing the ocean of open space between the living room and the foyer in about four strides.

He didn't hesitate to gather Viv in his strong arms, cradling her against his chest, and dang it, that T-shirt was really soft against her face. It was a testament to how mixed-up she was that she let him guide her to the leather couch and tuck her in against his side as he held her while softly crooning in his baritone that she'd heard in her sleep for aeons.

What was wrong with her that she was exactly where she wanted to be—in his arms? She should be pushing away and disappearing into her bedroom. No pressure, no love, no nothing.

"What's wrong, sweetheart?" he asked softly into her hair. "Bad day at work?"

"I wasn't at work," she shot back inanely, sniffling oh so attractively against his shoulder.

"Oh. Well, I wondered where you were when you weren't here."

"You weren't here either," she reminded him crossly. "So I went to dinner with Grace."

He pulled back, the expression on his face both confused and slightly alarmed. "Did we have plans that I forgot about or something? Because if so, I'm sorry. I didn't have anything on my calendar and my grandfather asked me to take him to the airport. I texted you."

He had? And how desperate would it appear to pull out her phone to check? Which was totally dumb anyway. It was obvious he was telling her the truth, which he didn't even have to do. God, she was such a mess. But after he'd disappeared this morning and then she'd come home to an empty house and…so what? He was here now, wasn't he? She was making a mountain out of a molehill.

"It's okay, we didn't have plans. You called it. Bad day at work," she said a bit more brightly as she latched on to his excuse that wasn't even a lie. Sales had been good, sure, but Cupcaked meant more to her than just profits. "I tried out a new recipe and it was a complete failure."

All smiles again, Jonas stroked her hair and then

laid a sweet kiss on her temple. "I hate days like that. What can I do to fix it?"

About a hundred suggestions sprang to her mind all at once, and every last one could easily be considered X-rated. But she couldn't bear to shift the current vibe into something more physical when Jonas was meeting a different kind of need, one she'd only nebulously identified at dinner. This was it in a nutshell—she wanted someone to be there for her, hold her and support her through the trials of life.

Why had she gotten so upset? Because Jonas hadn't fallen prostrate at her feet with declarations of undying love? They were essentially still in the early stages of their relationship, regardless of the label on it. Being married didn't automatically mean they were where Grace and her husband were. Maybe Viv and Jonas were taking a different route to get to the same destination and she was trying too hard.

Also known as the reason her last few relationships hadn't worked out.

"You're already fixing it," she murmured as his fingers drifted to her neck and lightly massaged.

Oh, God, that was a gloriously unfulfilled need, too. After a long day on her feet, just sitting here with Jonas as he worked her tired muscles counted as one of the highest points of pleasure she'd experienced at his hands. Her eyelids drifted closed and she floated.

"Did I wake you up this morning?" he asked after a few minutes of bliss.

"No. I was actually surprised to find that you were gone." Thank God he'd lulled her into a near coma. That admission had actually sounded a lot more casual than she would have expected, given how his absence had been lodged under skin like a saddle burr all day.

"That's good." He seemed a lot more relieved than the question warranted. "I'm not used to sleeping with someone and I was really worried that I'd mess with your schedule."

What schedule? "We slept in the same bed at your parents' house."

"Yeah, but that was over the weekend when no one had to get up and go to work. This is different. It's real life and I'm nothing if not conscious that you're here solely because I asked you to be. You deserve to sleep well."

Warmth gushed through her heart and made her feel entirely too sappy. What a thoroughly unexpected man she had married. "I did sleep well. Thank you for being concerned. But I think I slept so well because of how you treated me before I went to sleep. Not because you tiptoed well while getting dressed."

He did treat her like a queen. That was the thing she'd apparently forgotten. They were friends who cared about each other. Maybe he might eventually fall in love with her, but he certainly wouldn't if she kept being obsessive and reading into his every move.

Jonas chuckled. "Last night was pretty amazing.

I wasn't sure you thought so. I have to be honest and tell you that I was concerned I'd done something to make you angry and that's why you weren't here when I got home after taking my grandfather to the airport. I could have called him a car."

"No!" Horrified, she swiveled around to face him, even though it meant his wonderful hands slipped from her shoulders. "We just talked about no pressure and I was—well, I just thought because you weren't here…"

Ugh. How in the world was she supposed to explain that she'd gone out to dinner with Grace because of a hissy fit over something so ridiculous as Jonas not being here because he'd taken his grandfather to the airport? Maybe instead of using the excuse that she'd missed his text messages, she should tell him how she felt. Just flat out say, *Jonas, I'm in love with you.*

"We did talk about no pressure," Jonas threw out in a rush. "And I'm definitely not trying to add any. I like our relationship where it is. I like *you.* It's what makes the extra stuff so much better."

Extra stuff. She absorbed that for a second. Extra stuff like deeper feelings he didn't know he was going to uncover? Extra stuff like being there for each other?

"I value our friendship," she said cautiously, weighing out how honest she could be. How honest she wanted to be given how she managed to screw up even the simplest of relationship interactions.

And just as she was about to open her mouth and confess that she appreciated the extra stuff, too, maybe even tell him that she had a plethora of extra stuff that she could hardly hold inside, he smoothed a hand over her hair and grinned. "I know. I'm being all touchy-feely and that's not what we signed up for. Instead, let's talk about Cupcaked."

"Um…okay?" He'd literally switched gears so fast, she could scarcely keep up.

That was him being touchy-feely? Jonas wasn't one to be gushy about his feelings and usually erred on the side of being reserved; she knew that from the year of lunches and coffee. Clearly, he was uncomfortable with the direction of the discussion. She definitely should not add a level of weirdness, not on top of her storming in here and having a minor meltdown.

This was her relationship to make or break. All at once, it became so obvious what she should be focusing on here.

No, this wasn't practice for the next man she dated. She was practicing for *this* one. If she hoped to get to a point where they were both comfortable with declarations of love, she had to tread carefully. While she didn't think Jonas was going to divorce her if she moved too fast, neither did she have a good handle on how to be less intense.

She needed to back off. Way off. Otherwise, she was going to freak him out. And suddenly she could not fathom giving up this marriage under any circumstances.

"I'd love to talk about Cupcaked," she said with a smile. "Seems like you owe me some advice."

"Yes, exactly." His return smile bordered on relieved. "You've been so patient and I'm a selfish jerk for not focusing on your career when that's the one thing you're getting out of this deal."

"The sex is nice, too," she teased. Look at that. She could be cool.

Jonas shot her a wicked once-over. "That's what makes you so perfect. We can hang out as friends, but if I wanted to, say, slip my hand under your dress, you'd gladly climb in my lap for a little one-on-one time. It's the best."

She shrugged to cover how his compliment had thrilled her to the marrow. "I promised it wouldn't make things weird."

Now she'd stick to that. At the end of the day, Cupcaked *was* important to her. She'd just have to make sure that eventually Jonas realized that he was important to her, as well.

Jonas ducked out of a meeting on Friday with a guilty conscience. While he knew Viv would understand if he put off a thorough analysis of her business plan, he wasn't okay with ignoring his promise. Unfortunately, Park had come through with some amendments to the merger agreement Jonas had drafted, which had taken his time and attention for the whole of the week.

The moment he stepped outside the Kim Building, the sunshine raised his spirits. He was on his way to see his wife at Cupcaked, which oddly would mark the first time he'd graced the store since they'd gotten married. Before the wedding, he found excuses to drop by on a frequent basis. But now he didn't have to. The cupcake baker slept in his bed and if he wanted to see her, all he had to do was turn his head.

It was pretty great. Or at least that's what he'd been telling himself. In reality, the look on Viv's face when she'd told him she valued their friendship had been like a big fat wake-up call. Basically, she was telling him no pressure worked for her regardless of how hot he could get her with nothing more than a well-placed caress.

Well, that *was* great. He didn't have any desire to pressure her into anything. But he couldn't deny that he might like to put more structure around things. Would she think it was weird if he expected her to be his plus-one for events? His admin was planning a big party for the whole company to commemorate the anniversary of opening the Kim Americas branch. He wanted Viv by his side. But it was yet another favor. If they were dating instead of married he wouldn't think twice about asking her.

Everything was backward and weird and had been since that no-pressure discussion, which he'd initiated because he needed the boundaries. For no reason apparently. Viv so clearly wasn't charging over the imaginary lines he'd drawn in the sand. In fact, she'd drawn a few lines of her own. Yet how could he change those lines when Viv had gotten so prickly about the subject? In fact, she'd already tried to call off the intimate aspects of their relationship once. He needed to tread very carefully with her before he got in too deep for them both.

When he got to Cupcaked, the door was locked. Not open yet. He texted Viv that he was outside and within thirty seconds, she'd popped out of the kitchen and hurried to the plate-glass door with a cute smile.

"I didn't know you were coming by," she commented unnecessarily since he was well aware it was a surprise. After she let him in, she locked the door and turned, her brown hair shining in the sunlight that streamed through the glass.

Something was wrong with his lungs. He couldn't breathe. Or think. All he could do was soak in the most beautiful woman he'd ever seen in his life. And all of his good intentions designed to help her with her business flew out the window in a snap.

Without hesitation, he pulled her into his arms and kissed her. She softened instantly and the scent of vanilla and Viv wound through his senses, robbing him of the ability to reason, because the only thing he could think about was getting more of her against him.

Almost as if she'd read his mind, she opened

under his mouth, eagerly deepening the kiss, welcoming the broad stroke of his tongue with her own brand of heat. Slowly she licked into his mouth in kind, teasing him with little flutters of her fingers against his back.

That was not going to work. He wanted to feel her fingers against his flesh, not through the forty-seven layers of clothing between them.

Walking her backward, he half kissed, half maneuvered her until they reached the kitchen, and then he spun her through the swinging door to the more private area, where the entire city of Raleigh couldn't see them.

Her mouth was back on his without missing a beat, and he pushed her up against the metal counter, trapping her body with his. Her sweet little curves nestled into the planes of his body and he wasn't sure if he could stand how long it was taking to get her naked.

The zipper of her dress took three tries to find and then slid down easily, allowing him to actually push the fabric from her shoulders instead of ripping it, a near miracle. There was something about her that drove him to a place he didn't recognize, and it bothered him to be this crazy over her. But then her dress slipped off, puddling to the floor, and he forgot about everything but her as she unhooked her bra, throwing it to the ground on top of her dress.

Groaning, he looked his fill of her gorgeous breasts, scarcely able to believe how hard and pointy they were from nothing other than his gaze. Bending to capture one, he swirled his tongue around the perfection of her nipple and the sound she made shot through his erection like an arrow of heat.

"Hurry," she gasped. "I'm about to come apart."

Oh, well, that was something he'd very much like to witness. In a flash, he pushed her panties to her ankles and boosted her up on the counter. Spreading her legs wide, he brushed a thumb through her crease and, yes, she was so ready for him.

She bucked and rolled against his fingers, her eyes darkening with the pleasure he was giving her, and he wanted her more than anything he could recall. As much as he'd like to do any number of things to bring her to climax, there was one clear winner. Ripping out of his own clothes in record time, he stepped back between her thighs and hissed as she nipped at his shoulder.

"Tell me you have a condom," she commanded, and then smiled as he held it up between his fingers.

He'd stashed a couple in his wallet and he really didn't want to examine that particular foresight right now. Instead, he wanted to examine the wonders of Viv and sheathed himself as fast as humanly possible, notching himself at the slick entrance to her channel. Her wet heat welcomed him, begged him to come inside, but he paused to kiss her because that was one of his favorite parts.

Their tongues tangled and he got a little lost in the kiss. She didn't. She wrapped her legs around him, heels firm against his butt, and pushed him forward, gasping as he slammed into her. So that's how she wanted it. Two could play that game.

He engulfed her in his arms and braced her for a demanding rhythm, then gave it to her. She took each and every thrust eagerly, her mouth working the flesh at his throat, his ear, nipping sensuously. *He* was the one about to come apart.

Viv flew through his soul, winging her essence into every diameter of his body. Wiggling a hand between their slick bodies, he fingered her at the source of her pleasure, gratified when she cried out. Her release crashed against his, shocking him with both the speed and intensity.

She slumped against him, still quaking as she held on. He was busy losing the entire contents of his body as everything inside rushed out in a flash to fill her. Fanciful to be sure since there was a barrier preventing anything of the sort. But she'd wrung him out, taken everything and more, and he couldn't have stopped the train as it barreled down the track, even if he wanted to. Why would he want to?

He turned his head, seeking her lips, and there they were, molding to his instantly. Viv was amazing, a woman he liked, cared for deeply even, and they had the most spectacular chemistry. He could hardly fathom how much he still wanted her four seconds after having her. It was everything he said he wanted.

Except the warmth in his chest that had nothing to do with sex wasn't supposed to be there. He wasn't an idiot. He knew what was happening. He'd let her in, pretending that being friends gave him a measure of protection against falling for her. Instead, he'd managed to do the one thing he'd sworn he'd never do—develop feelings for someone who didn't return them.

This was a huge problem, one he didn't have a good solution for. One he could never let her know he was facing because he'd promised not to pressure her.

Best thing would be to ignore it. It wasn't happening if he didn't acknowledge it. And then he wouldn't be lying to her or dishonoring the pact he'd made with his friends, neither of which could ever happen. If he didn't nurture these fledging tendrils of disaster that wound through his chest, he could kill them before they ruined everything.

Actually, the best thing would be to stop being around Viv so much. *Without* letting on to her that he was deliberately creating distance.

The thought hurt. But it was necessary for his sanity.

Nine

Jonas helped Viv off the metal countertop that she'd have to bleach within an inch of its life and pray the fourteen different health-code violations never came to light.

It had been worth it. Whenever Jonas got like that, so into her and excited and feverish as if he'd die if he didn't have her that instant…that was the best part of this fake marriage. Men were never that gaga over her. Except this one. And she secretly loved it. She couldn't tell him. What would she say?

Slow and steady wins the race, she reminded herself. Not-Clingy was her new middle name and she was going to own it. Even if it killed her not to blubber all over him about how it was so beautiful it hurt when he was inside her.

They spent a few minutes setting their clothes back to rights, no small feat without a mirror. She gladly helped Jonas locate his missing tie and then buttoned his suit jacket for him when he forgot.

"Gorgeous," she commented after slipping the last button into its slot and perusing the final product of her husband in his power suit that she immediately wanted to strip him out of again.

He grinned. "Yes, you are."

Great, now she was blushing, judging by the prickles in her cheeks. Dead giveaway about the things going on inside that she'd rather keep a secret.

"Now, stop distracting me," he continued. "I'm here to get started on my promise to review your books. Lead me to them."

Oh. For some reason, she'd thought he'd come by strictly to have an explosive sexual encounter in her bakery. But in reality, he was here for business reasons. That took a little of the wind from her sails though it shouldn't have. Of course he'd honor his promise to help her, despite absolutely no prompting on her part. "Sure, my office is in the back. We can squeeze in there."

She led him to the tiny hole in the wall where she paid bills and ordered inventory. It wasn't much, not like the Kim Building, where Jonas had an entire office suite expressly designed for the CEO. But she wasn't running a billion-dollar electronics company here, and they both knew that.

He didn't complain about the lack of comfort and space, easily sliding into the folding chair she pulled from behind the door and focusing on her with his dark eyes. "Let me see your balance sheet."

Dutifully, she keyed up her accounting software and ran the report, then pushed the monitor of her ancient computer toward him so he could see it. His gaze slid down the columns and back up again. Within a moment, he'd reviewed the entire thing and then launched into a dizzying speech about how her asset column was blah blah and her inventory was blah blah something else. After five minutes of nodding and understanding almost nothing of what he said, she held up a hand.

"Jonas, while I appreciate your attention on this, you lost me back around 'leveraging your cash.' Can we take a step back and focus on the goal of this?"

She knew what her goal was. Spend time with Jonas. But clearly he'd taken the idea of helping her seriously.

"Sure, sorry." He looked chagrined and adorable as he ran a hand through his hair. "I shouldn't have gone so deep into financial strategy that quickly. Maybe I should ask you what *your* goal is since your career is the most important thing to you. What do you want to see happen with Cupcaked?"

Oh, yeah, right. Her career. The thing she'd sold

to him as the reason she didn't date. "I haven't really thought about it."

Should she be thinking about it? She wasn't rich by any stretch, but she made enough and got to bake cupcakes for a living. What else was there?

"Okay." His smile broadened. "I hear you saying that you need help coming up with a five-year plan. Part of that should include a robust marketing strategy and expansion."

Expansion? Her eyebrows lifted almost by themselves. "Are you suggesting I could become a chain?"

The idea seemed so far-fetched. She just made cupcakes and had no ambitions beyond being able to recognize regular customers. But she didn't hate the idea of seeing more Cupcaked signs around Raleigh. Maybe even in Chapel Hill or by the university. The thought of owning a mini-cupcake empire made her smile. Poor substitute for Jonas. But not a terrible one.

"I'm not suggesting it. I'm flat out saying if that's what you want, I will make it happen for you. Sky's the limit, Mrs. Kim." He waggled his brows. "You should take as much advantage of me as you possibly can. Ask for anything."

Mrs. Kim. What if she told him that she'd like to ask him to call her that for the rest of her life? What would he say?

Before she could open her mouth, he launched into another long litany of things to consider for her shop and his gleeful tone told her he was having fun helping her think through the items that might appear on her five-year plan. They talked about any number of ideas from branded cupcake mix to be sold in grocery stores to licensing her flavors to other cupcake bakeries.

Frankly, the discussion was fun for her, too. Partially because she was having it with Jonas and she loved watching his mind churn through the possibilities. But she couldn't deny a certain anticipation regarding the leaps and bounds Cupcaked could take through the doors her husband might open for her.

Camilla popped in to say hi and make sure Viv was okay with her opening the bakery to customers. Viv nodded her assent and dove back into the fascinating concept of franchising, of which Jonas admitted having only a rudimentary knowledge, but he knew way more than she did. She wanted to know more.

His phone rang and he lifted a finger in the universal "one minute" gesture, jabbering away to the caller with a bunch of terms that sounded vaguely legal. Eventually, he ended the call and stood.

"I'm so sorry, but I have to get back to the world of electronics."

She waved off his apology. "You've been here for two hours. I know you're busy. I should give Camilla a hand anyway. If today is anything like the rest of the week, she'll need the help."

Jonas laid a scorching kiss on her and left. Dazed and more than a little hot and bothered, she lost herself in cupcakes until the day got away from her. As planned, she and Jonas went to dinner at her parents' house that night. Given that he shot her smoking-hot glances when he thought no one was watching, and her sisters were nothing if not eagle-eyed when it came to potential gossip, she didn't think they had anything to worry about when it came to revelations about the nature of their marriage.

Or rather, the revelations weren't going to be publicized to the rest of the world. Just to Jonas. As soon as she figured out when she could start clueing him in to the idea that friendship wasn't the only thing happening between them, of course. This was the problem with playing it cool. She wasn't sure when to bring up concepts like *love*, *forever* and *no divorce*.

She bided her time and didn't utter a peep when Jonas carried her to his bed after the successful dinner with her parents. He spent extra time pleasuring her, claiming that tomorrow was Saturday so she had plenty of opportunity to sleep later. Not that she was complaining about his attention. Or anything else, for that matter. Her life was almost perfect.

On Monday, she learned exactly how many people in the business world jumped when her husband said jump. By nine o'clock, she had appointments lined up every day for the entire week with accounting people, retail space experts and a pastry chef who had ties with the Food Network. A marketing consultant arrived shortly thereafter and introduced herself as Franca, then parked herself in Viv's office, apparently now a permanent part of her staff, as she'd informed Mrs. Kim, courtesy of Mr. Kim.

Franca lived to talk, as best Viv could work out between marathon strategy sessions that filled nearly every waking hour of the day. And some of the hours Viv would have normally said were for sleeping. At midnight, Franca sent a detailed list of the short-term and long-term goals that they'd discussed and asked Viv to vet it thoroughly because once she approved, the list would form the basis of Cupcaked's new five-year plan. Which would apparently be carved in stone.

By Friday, Viv hadn't spent more than five minutes with Jonas. They slept in the same bed, but sometimes he climbed into it well after she had, which was quite a feat since she hadn't hit the sheets until 1:00 a.m. most nights. He'd claimed her busyness came at a great time for him because he was able to focus on the merger with Park Industries without feeling guilty for ignoring her. The hours bled into days and she'd never been so exhausted in her life.

It sucked. Except for the part where sometimes Jonas texted her funny memes about ships passing in the night or had a dozen tulips delivered to the shop to commemorate their one-month anniversary. Once he popped up with Chinese takeout for dinner as a "forced" break for them both. He gave her his fortune cookie and told her a story about how one of the ladies in his procurement department had gone into labor during a meeting. Those stolen moments meant the world to her because she could almost believe that he missed her as much as she missed him.

The pièce de résistance came when the pastry chef she'd met with a couple of weeks ago contacted her via Franca to let her know that he'd loved her cupcakes and gotten her a spot on one of the cupcake shows on the Food Network. Agape, Viv stared at Franca as the tireless woman reeled off the travel plans she'd made for Viv to fly to Los Angeles.

"I can't go to Los Angeles," Viv insisted with a head shake. "I have a business to run."

Franca tapped her phone on Viv's new desk. "Which will become nationally known once you appear on the show."

She'd had Viv's office completely redone and expanded at Jonas's expense and the top-of-the-line computer that had replaced the old one now recessed underneath the surface of the desk with the click of a button. It was very slick and gave them a lot more working space, which Franca used frequently, as she spread brochures and promo items galore across the top of it at least twice a week.

"How long would I be gone?" Viv asked. Josie and Camilla had never run the bakery by themselves for a whole day, let alone several. They needed her. Or did they? She was often in the back strategizing with Franca anyway. They had four or five irons in the fire at any given time and the woman was indefatigable when it came to details. There was literally nothing she couldn't organize or plan and often took on more of a personal assistant role for Viv.

"Depends on whether you make the first cut." Franca shrugged and flipped her ponytail behind her back, a move she made when she was about to get serious. "It's a competition. You lose the first round, you come home. You win, you stay. I would advise you to win."

Viv made a face. "You're talking days."

"Sure. I hope so anyway. We're going to launch the new website with online ordering at the same time. It'll be an amazing kick start to the virtual storefront."

Sagging a little, Viv gave herself about four seconds to pretend she was going to refuse when in reality, she couldn't pass up the opportunity. It really didn't matter if she won or not because it was free advertising and all it would cost her was some time away from Jonas. Whom she rarely saw awake anyway.

"When do I leave?"

Franca grinned like she'd known the direction Viv would end up going the whole time. "I'll get the rest of the arrangements settled and let you know."

With a nod, Viv texted the news to Jonas, who instantly responded with at least four exclamation marks and a *congrats* in all caps. Funny, they were basically back to being friends with no benefits, thanks to her stupid career. She had all the success she'd lied to Jonas about wanting and none of the happiness that she'd pretended would come along with it.

Worse, if she hadn't been so busy, she'd be sitting around the condo by herself as Jonas worked his own fingers to the bone. This was really, really not the marriage she'd signed up for.

Or rather it was absolutely the one she'd agreed to but not the one she wanted.

The day before she was supposed to fly to Los Angeles for the taping, Viv came home early to pack. Shockingly, Jonas was sitting on the couch still decked out in his gorgeous suit but on the phone, as he nearly always was anytime she'd been in the same room with him lately.

For half a second, she watched him, soaking in his pretty mouth as it formed words. Shuddered as she recalled what that mouth could do to her when he put his mind to it. God, she missed him. In the short amount of time they'd been married, they'd gone from zero to sixty to zero again. She'd prefer a hundred and twenty.

She waved, loath to interrupt him, but before she could skirt past him to her bedroom, where her clothes still were since she'd never really "moved in" to Jonas's room, he snagged her by the hips and settled her on the couch near him as he wrapped up his phone call.

Tossing his phone on the glass-and-steel conglomeration that he called a coffee table, he contemplated her with the sort of attention she hadn't experienced in a long while. It was delicious.

"You're going to LA in the morning?" he said by way of greeting, and picked up her hand to hold it in his, brushing his thumb across her knuckles.

"Yeah. I don't know for how long. Franca left the plane ticket open-ended." The little strokes of his thumb stirred something inside that had been dormant for a million years. He'd been so distant lately. Dare she hope that they might be coming back together?

No reason she had to let him be the instigator. She lifted his hand to her mouth and kissed it, but he pulled away and sat back on the couch. "That sounds like fun. I hope you have a good time."

Cautiously, she eyed him. Why had he caught her before she left the room if he hadn't been after spending time with her? "Is everything okay? I wasn't expecting you to be here."

"I…came home on purpose. To see you," he admitted. "Before you left."

Her heart did a funny a little dance. But then why all the weird hot and cold? He obviously cared about her—but how much? Enough? She had no idea because they never talked about what was really going on here.

It was high time they had it out. She was leaving for LA in the morning and they rarely saw each other. She had to make this small opportunity work.

"I'm glad. I missed you." There. It was out in the open.

But he just smiled without a hint of anything. "I miss hanging out with you, too. We haven't had coffee in ages."

Or sex. The distinction between the two was legion and she didn't think for a minute that he'd misspoken or forgotten that they'd been intimate. It was a deliberate choice of words. "We haven't had a coffee relationship in ages."

His expression didn't change. "I know. It's been crazy. We're both so busy."

"By design, feels like."

That got a reaction, but why, she couldn't fathom. She watched as unease filtered through his gaze and he shifted positions on the couch, casually folding one leg over the other but also moving away from her. "We're both workaholics, that's for sure."

"I'm not," she corrected. "Not normally. But I've been dropped into an alternate reality where Franca drives me fourteen hours a day to reach these lofty goals that don't represent what I really want out of life."

Jonas frowned, his gaze sweeping over her in assessment. "You're finally getting your career off the ground. She's been keeping me apprised and I've been pleased with the direction she's taking you. But if you're not, we should discuss it. I can hire a different marketing expert, one that's more in line—"

"It's not the direction of the marketing," she broke

in before he called in yet another career savant who would be brilliant at taking her away from her husband. "It's that I was happier when Cupcaked was a little bakery on Jones Street and we had sex in the foyer."

Something flitted through his gaze that she wished felt more like an invitation. Because she would have stripped down right here, right now if that had gotten the reaction she'd hoped for. Instead, his expression had a huge heaping dose of caution. "We agreed that we'd take that part as it came. No pressure. You're focusing on your career, just like I am. If Franca's not guiding you toward the right next level, then what do you want her to do?"

"I want her to go away!" Viv burst out. "She's exhausting and so chipper and can do more from 10:00 p.m. to midnight than a general, two single moms and the president combined. I want to have dinner with you, and lie in bed on a Saturday morning and watch cartoons with my head on your shoulder. I want you to rip my dress at the seams because you're so eager to get me naked. Most of all, I don't want to think about cupcakes."

But he was shaking his head. "That's not me. I'm not the kind of guy who rips a woman's dress off."

"But you are. You did," she argued inanely because what a stupid thing to say. He was totally that man and she loved it when he was like that. "I don't understand why we were so hot and heavy and then you backed off."

There came another shadow through his gaze that darkened his whole demeanor. "Because we're friends and I'm nothing if not interested in preserving that relationship."

"I am, too," she shot back a little desperately. This conversation was sliding away from her at an alarming pace, turning into something it shouldn't be, and she wasn't sure how that had happened. Or how to fix it. "But I'm also not happy just being friends. I love the text messages and I'm thrilled with what you've done for my business. But it's not enough."

"What are you saying?" he asked cautiously, his expression blank.

"That I want a real marriage. A family. I want more than just cupcakes."

Jonas let the phrase soak through him. Everything inside shifted, rolling over. In six words, Viv had reshaped the entire dynamic between them, and the effects might be more destructive than a nuclear bomb.

His chest certainly felt like one had gone off inside. While he'd been fighting to keep from treating Viv to a repeat of the dress-ripping incident, she'd been quietly planning to cut him off at the knees. Apparently he'd been creating distance for no reason.

Viv's gorgeous face froze when he didn't immediately respond. But what was he supposed to say?

Oh, that's right. *What the hell?*

"Viv, I've known you for over a year. We've been married for almost five weeks. For pretty much the entire length of our acquaintance, you've told me how important your career is to you. I have never once heard you mention that you wanted a family. Can you possibly expand on that statement?"

The weird vibe went even more haywire and he had the impression she regretted what she'd said. Then, she dropped her head into her hands, covering her eyes for a long beat. The longer she hid from him, the more alarmed he got. What was she afraid he'd see?

"Not much to expand on," she mumbled to her palms. "I like cupcakes, but I want a husband and a family, too."

Which was pretty much what she'd just said, only rephrased in such a way as to still not make any sense. "Let me ask this a different way. Why have you never told me this? I thought we were friends."

Yeah, that was a little bitterness fighting to get free.

How well did he really know the woman he'd married if this was just now coming out after all this time? After all the intimacies that they'd shared?

The lick of temper uncurling inside was completely foreign. He'd asked her to marry him strictly because he'd been sure—*positive* even—that she wasn't the slightest bit interested in having a long-term relationship.

Otherwise, he never would have asked her to do this favor. Never would have let himself start to care more than he should have.

His anger fizzled. He could have been more forth-coming with his own truths but hadn't for reasons that he didn't feel that self-righteous about all at once.

"I never told you because it...never came up." Guilt flickered in her tone and when she lifted her face from her hands, it was there in her expression, too. "I'm only telling you now because you asked."

Actually, he hadn't. He'd been sorting through her comments about the marketing consultant he'd hired, desperately trying to figure out if Viv and Franca just didn't get along or if the references he'd received regarding the consultant's brilliance had been em-bellished. Instead, she'd dropped a whole different issue in his lap. One that was knifing through his chest like a dull machete.

Viv wanted a real husband. A family. This fake marriage was in her way. *Jonas* was in her way. It was shattering. Far more than he would have said.

He didn't want to lose her. But neither could he keep her, not at the expense of giving her what she really wanted. Obviously he should have given more weight to the conversation they'd had at his parents' house about love being a good basis for marriage. Clearly that was what she wanted from a husband.

And he couldn't give her that, nor was she ask-ing him to. He'd made a promise that he'd never let a woman have enough sway to affect his emotions. Judging by the swirl of confusion beneath his breast-bone, it was already too late for that.

If she just hadn't said anything. He could have

kept pretending that the solution to all his problems was to keep her busy until he figured out how to make all his inappropriate feelings go away.

But this…he couldn't ignore what he knew was the right thing to do.

"Viv." Vising his forehead between his fingers, he tried like hell to figure out how they'd gotten so off track. "You've been telling me for over a year that your career sucked up all your time and that's why you didn't date. How were you planning to meet said husband?"

"I don't know," she shot back defensively. "And cupcakes are important to me. It's just not the only thing, and this marathon of business-plan goals kind of solidified that fact for me. I love the idea of sharing my recipes with a bigger block of customers. But not at the expense of the kind of marriage I think would make me happy. I want—need—to back off."

Back off. From him, she meant. Jonas blinked as something wrenched loose in his chest, and it felt an awful lot like she'd gripped his heart in her fingers, then twisted until it fell out. "I understand. You deserve to have the kind of marriage you want and I can't give that to you."

Her face froze, going so glacial all at once he scarcely recognized her.

"You've never thought about having a real marriage?" she asked in a whisper.

Not once. Until now. And now it was all he could think about. What was a real marriage to her? Love, honor and cherish for the rest of her days? He could do two out of three. Would she accept that? Then he could keep her friendship, keep this marriage and… how crappy was that, to even contemplate how far he could take this without breaking his word to anyone? It was ridiculous. They should have hashed out this stuff long ago. Like before they got married. And he would have if she'd told him that she harbored secret dreams of hearts and googly eyes. Too bad that kind of stuff led to emotional evisceration when everything went south.

Like now.

"Viv." She shifted to look at him, apparently clueing in that he had something serious to say. "I married you specifically because I have no intention of having a real marriage. It was deliberate."

Something that looked a lot like pain flashed through her gaze. "Because I'm not real marriage material?"

A sound gurgled in his throat as he got caught between a vehement denial and an explanation that hopefully didn't make him sound like an ass.

"Not because you're unlovable or something." God, what was wrong with him? He was hurting her with his thoughtlessness. She'd spilled her guts to him, obviously because she trusted him with the truth, and the best he could do was smash her dreams? "I care about you. That's why we're having this conversation, which we should have had a long time ago. I never told you about Marcus."

Eyes wide, she shook her head but stayed silent as he spit out the tale of his friend who had loved and lost and then never recovered. When he wound it up with the tragedy and subsequent pact, she blinked away a sheen of tears that he had no idea what to do with.

"So you, Warren and Hendrix are all part of this... club?" she asked. "The Never Going to Fall in Love club?"

It sounded silly when she said it like that. "It's not a club. We swore solemn vows and I take that seriously."

She nodded once, but confusion completely screwed up her beautiful face. "I see. Instead of having something wonderful with a life partner, you intend to stick to a promise you made under duress a decade ago."

"No," he countered quietly. "I intend to stand by a promise I made, period. Because that's who I am. It's a measure of my ethical standards. A testament to the kind of man I want to be."

"Alone? That's the kind of man you want to be?"

"That's not fair." Why was she so concerned about his emotional state all at once? "I don't want to be alone. That's why I like being married to you so much. We have fun together. Eat dinner. Watch TV."

"Not lately," she said pointedly, and it was an arrow through his heart. If he was going to throw around his ethics like a blunt instrument, then he couldn't very well pretend he didn't know what she meant.

"Not lately," he agreed. "I'd like to say it's because we've both been busy. But that's not the whole truth. I...started to get a little too attached to you. Distance was necessary."

The sheen was back over her eyes. "Because of the pact. You've been pulling back on purpose."

He nodded. The look on her face was killing him, and he'd like nothing more than to yank her into his arms and tell her to forget that nonsense. Because he wanted his friend back. His lover. His everything.

But he couldn't. In the most unfair turnabout, he'd told her about the pact and instead of her running in the other direction like a lot of women, *he* was the one shutting down. "It was the only way I could keep you as my wife and honor the promises I made to myself and to my friends. And to you. I said no pressure. I meant to keep it that way. Which still stands, by the way."

She laughed, but he didn't think it was because she found any of this funny. "I think this is about the lowest-pressure marriage on the planet."

"You misunderstand. I'm saying no pressure to stay married."

Her gaze cut to him and he took the quick, hard punch to the gut in stride without letting on to her how difficult it had been to utter those words.

Take them back. Right now.

But he couldn't.

"Jonas, we can't get divorced. You'd lose your grandfather's support to take over his role."

The fact that she'd even consider that put the whole conversation in perspective. They were friends who cared about each other. Which meant he had to let her go, no matter how hard it was. "I know. But it's not fair to you to stay in this marriage given that you want something different."

"I do want something different," she agreed quietly. "I have to go to LA. I can't think about any of this right now."

He let her fingers slip from his, and when she shut herself in her bedroom, the quiet click of the door burst through his chest like a gunshot to the heart. He wished he felt like congratulating himself on his fine upstanding character, but all he felt like doing was crawling into bed and throwing a blanket over his head. The absence of Viv left a cold, dark place inside that even a million blankets couldn't warm.

Ten

The trip to LA was a disaster. Oh, the cooking show was fine. She won the first round. But Viv hated having to fake smile, hated pretending her marriage wasn't fake, hated the fakeness of baking on camera with a script full of fake dialogue.

There was nothing real about her, apparently. And it had been slowly sapping her happiness away until she couldn't stand it if one more person called her Mrs. Kim. Why had she changed her name? Even that was temporary until some ambiguous point in the future.

Well, there was one thing that was real. The way she felt about Jonas, as evidenced by the numbness inside that she carried 24/7. Finally, she had someone to care about and *he* cared about *her*. Yay. He cared so much that he was willing to let her out of the favor of being married to him so she could *find someone else*.

How ironic that she'd ended up exactly where she'd intended to be. All practiced up for her next relationship, except she didn't want to move on. She wanted Jonas, just like she had for over a year, and she wanted him to feel the same about her.

The cooking show, or rather the more correctly labeled entertainment venue disguised as a cupcake battle, wrapped up the next day. Viv won the final round and Franca cheered from the sidelines, pointing to her phone, where she was presumably checking out the stats on Cupcaked's new digital storefront. Every time the show's camera zoomed in on Viv's face, they put a graphic overlay on the screen with her name and the name of her cupcake bakery. Whatever results that had produced made Franca giddy, apparently.

It was all too overwhelming. None of this was what she wanted. Instead of cooking shows, Viv should have been spending fourteen hours a day working on her marriage. The what-ifs were all she could think about.

On the plane ride home, Franca jabbered about things like click-through rates, branding and production schedules. They'd already decided to outsource the baking for the digital storefront because Viv's current setup couldn't handle the anticipated volume. Judging by the numbers Franca was throwing out, it had been a good decision.

Except for the part where none of this was what Viv wanted. And it was high time she fixed that.

When she got home, she drafted a letter to Franca thanking her for all of her hard work on Viv's behalf but explaining that her career was not in fact the most important thing in her life, so Franca's services were no longer needed. The improvements to Cupcaked were great and Viv intended to use the strategies that they'd both developed. But she couldn't continue to invest so much energy into her business, not if she hoped to fix whatever was broken in Jonas's head that made him think that saying a few words a decade ago could ever compare with the joy of having the kind of marriage she'd watched her sisters experience. Viv had been shuffled to the side once again and she wasn't okay with that.

Jonas came home late. No surprise there. That seemed to be the norm. But she was not prepared to see the lines of fatigue around his eyes. Or the slight shock flickering through his expression when he caught sight of her sitting on the couch.

"Hey," he called. "Didn't know you were back."

"Surprise." Served him right. "Sit down so we can talk."

Caution drenched his demeanor and he took his time slinging his leather bag over the back of a chair. "Can it wait? I have a presentation to the board tomorrow and I'd like to go over—"

"You're prepared," she told him and patted the cushion next to her. "I've known you for a long time and I would bet every last cupcake pan I own that you've been working on that PowerPoint every spare second for days. You're going to kill it. Sit."

It was a huge kick that he obeyed, and she nearly swooned when the masculine scent of her husband washed over her. He was too far away to touch, but she could rectify that easily. When it was time. She was flying a little blind here, but she did know one thing—she was starting over from scratch. No familiar ingredients. No beloved pan. The oven wasn't even heated up yet. But she had her apron on and the battle lines drawn. Somehow, she needed to bake a marriage until it came out the way she liked.

"What's up? How was the show?" he asked conversationally, but strictly to change the subject, she was pretty sure.

"Fine. I won. It was fabulous. I fired Franca."

That got his attention. "What? Why would you do that?"

"Because she's too good for me. She needs to go help someone run an empire." She smiled as she gave Jonas a once-over. "You should hire her, in fact."

"Maybe I will." His dark eyes had a flat, guarded quality that she didn't like. While she knew academically that she had to take a whole different track with him, it was another thing entirely to be this close but yet so far.

"Jonas, we have to finish our conversation. The one from the other day."

"I wasn't confused about which one you meant." A brief lift of his lips encouraged her to continue, but then the shield between them snapped back into place. "You've decided to go."

"No. I'm not going anywhere." Crossing her arms so she couldn't reach out to him ranked as one of the hardest things she'd done. But it was necessary to be clear about this without adding a bunch of other stuff into the mix. "I said I was going to do you this favor and as strongly as you believe in keeping your word, it inspires me to do the same. I'm here for the duration."

Confusion replaced the guardedness and she wasn't sure which one she liked less. "You're staying? As my wife?"

"And your friend." She shrugged. "Nothing you said changed anything for me. I still want the marriage I envision and I definitely won't get that if I divorce you."

Jonas flinched and a million different things sprang into the atmosphere between them. "You're not thinking clearly. You'll never meet someone who can give you what you want if you stay married to me."

"For a smart man, you're being slow to catch on." The little noise of disgust sounded in her chest before she could check it. But *men*. So dense. "I want a real marriage with *you*, not some random guy off the street. What do you think we've been doing here but building this into something amazing? I know you want to honor your word to your friends—"

"Viv." The quiet reverberation of her name stopped her cold and she glanced at him. He'd gone so still that her pulse tumbled. "It's not just a promise I made to my friends. I have no room in my life for a real marriage. The pact was easy for me to make. It's not that I swore to never fall in love. It's that I refuse to. It's a destructive emotion that leads to more destruction. That's not something I'm willing to chance."

Her mouth unhinged and she literally couldn't make a sound to save her life. Something cold swept along her skin as she absorbed his sincerity.

"Am I making sense?" he asked after a long pause.

That she could answer easily. "None. Absolutely no sense."

His mouth firmed into a long line and he nodded. "It's a hard concept for someone like you who wants to put your faith and trust in someone else. I don't. I can't. I've built something from nothing, expanded Kim Electronics into a billion-dollar enterprise in the American market, and I'm poised to take that to the next level. I cannot let a woman nor the emotions one might introduce ruin everything."

She'd only thought nothing could make her colder than his opening statement. But the ice forming from this last round of crazy made her shiver. "You're lumping *me* in that category? *I'm* this nebulous entity known as 'woman' who might go Helen of Troy on your business? I don't even know what to say to that."

Grimly, he shook his head. "There's nothing to say. Consider this from my perspective. I didn't even know you wanted anything beyond your career until a couple of days ago. What else don't I know? I can't take that risk. Not with you."

"What?" Her voice cracked. "You're saying you don't trust me because I didn't blather on about hearts and flowers from the first moment I met you?"

Pathetic. Not-clingy hadn't worked. In fact, it might have backfired. If she'd just told him how she felt from the beginning, she could have used the last five weeks to combat his stupid pact.

Something white-hot and angry rose up in her throat. Seriously, this was so unfair. She couldn't be herself with *anyone*. Instead there were all these rules and games and potholes and loopholes, none of which she understood or cared about.

"Viv." He reached out and then jerked his hand back before touching her, as if he'd only just realized that they weren't in a place where that was okay. "It's not a matter of trust. It's…me. I can't manage how insane you make me."

She eyed him, sniffling back a tsunami of tears. "So now I make you crazy? Listen, buster, I'm not the one talking crazy here—"

A strangled sound stopped her rant. Jonas shook his head, clearly bemused. "Not crazy. Give me a break. I was expecting you to walk out the door, not grill me on things I don't know how to explain. Just stop for a second."

His head dropped into his hands and he massaged his temples.

"Insane and crazy are the same thing."

"I mean how much I want you!" he burst out. "All the time. You make me insane with wanting to touch you, and roll into you in the middle of the night to hold you. Kiss you until you can't breathe. So, yeah, I'll give you that. It makes me crazy. In this case, it does mean the same thing."

Reeling, she stared at him, dumbstruck, numb, so off balance she couldn't figure out how to make her brain work. What in the world was wrong with *any* of that?

"I don't understand what you're telling me, Jonas."

"It's already way too much." He threw up his hands. "How much worse will it get? I refuse to let my emotions control me like that."

This was awful. He was consciously rejecting the concept of allowing anything deeper to grow between them. Period. No questions asked. She let that reality seep into her soul as her nails dug into her palms with little pinpricks of pain that somehow centered her. If this was his decision, she had to find a way to live with it.

"So, what happens next?" she whispered. "I don't want a divorce. Do you?"

At that, he visibly crumpled, folding in on himself as if everything hurt. She knew the feeling.

"I can't even answer that." His voice dipped so low that she could scarcely make it out. "My grandfather asked me to come to Korea as soon as possible. He got some bad news from his doctor and he's retiring earlier than expected."

"Oh, no." Viv's hand flew to her mouth as she took in the devastation flitting through Jonas's expression. "Is he going to be okay?"

"I don't know. He wants you to come. How can I ask that of you?" His gaze held a world of pain and indecision and a million other things that her own expression probably mirrored. "It's not fair to you."

This was where the rubber met the road. He wasn't asking her to go, nor would he. He was simply stating facts and giving the choice to her. If she wanted to claim a real marriage for herself, she had to stand by her husband through thick and thin, sickness and health, vows of honor and family emergencies.

This was the ultimate test. Did she love Jonas enough to ignore her own needs in order to fulfill his? If nothing else, it was her sole opportunity to do and be whatever she wanted in a relationship. Her marriage, her rules. If she had a mind to cling like Saran Wrap to Jonas, it was her right.

In what was probably the easiest move of the entire conversation, she reached out to lace her fingers with his and held on tight. "If you strip everything else away, I'm still your wife. Your grandfather could still pass his support to someone else if he suspects something isn't right between us. If you want me to go, I'll go."

Clearly equal parts shocked and grateful, he stared at her. "Why would you do that for me?"

She squared her shoulders. "Because I said I would."

No matter how hard it would be.

Jonas kept sneaking glances at Viv as she slept in the reclined leather seat opposite his. She'd smiled for nearly ten minutes after claiming a spot aboard the Kim private jet that Grandfather had sent to Raleigh to fetch them. It was fun to watch her navigate the spacious fuselage and interact with the attentive staff, who treated her like royalty. Obviously his grandfather had prepped them in advance.

But after the initial round of post-takeoff champagne, Viv had slipped back into the morose silence that cloaked them both since their conversation. He'd done everything in his power to drive her away so he didn't hurt her and what had she done? Repacked the suitcase that she'd just pulled off a conveyor belt at the airport hours before and announced she was coming with him to Korea. No hesitation.

What was he going to do with her?

Not much, apparently. The distance between them was nearly palpable. Viv normally had this vibe of openness about her as if she'd never met a stranger and he could talk to her about anything. Which he had, many times. Since he'd laid down the law about what kind of marriage they could have in that desperate bid to stop the inevitable, there might as well have been an impenetrable steel wall between them.

Good. That was perfect. Exactly what he'd hoped for.

He hated it.

This purgatory was exactly what he deserved, though. If Viv wasn't being her beautiful, kind, amazing self, there was no chance of his emotions engaging. Or rather, engaging further. He was pretty sure there was a little something already stirring around inside. Okay a lot of something, but if he could hold on to that last 50 percent, he could still look Warren and Hendrix in the eye next time they were in the same room.

If he could just cast aside his honor, all of this would be so much easier.

Seoul's Incheon Airport spread out beneath them in all its dazzling silvery glory, welcoming him back to Korea. He appreciated the birthplace of his father and the homeland of his grandfather. Seoul was a vibrant city rich in history with friendly people who chattered in the streets as they passed. It was cosmopolitan in a way that Raleigh could never be, but Jonas preferred the more laid-back feel of his own homeland.

"It's beautiful," Viv commented quietly as the limo Grandfather had sent wound through the streets thronged with people and vehicles.

"I'll take you a few places while we're here," he

offered. "You shouldn't miss Gyeongbokgung Palace."

They could walk through Insa-dong, the historic neighborhood that sold art and food, then maybe breeze by the Seoul Tower. He could perfectly envision the delighted smile on her face as she discovered the treasures of the Eastern world that comprised a portion of his lineage. Maybe he'd even find an opportunity to take her hand as they strolled, and he could pretend everything was fine between them.

But Viv was already shaking her head. "You don't have to do that. I don't need souvenirs. You're here for your grandfather and I'm here for you."

That made him feel like crap. But it was an inescapable fact that she'd come because he needed her. Warmth crowded into his chest as he gazed at her, the beauty of Seoul rushing past the limousine window beyond the glass.

"Why?" he asked simply, too overcome to be more articulate.

Her gaze sought his, and for a brief moment, her normal expressiveness spilled onto her face. Just as quickly, she whisked it away. "No matter what, you're still my friend."

The sentiment caught in his throat. Her sacrifice and the unbelievable willingness to be there for him would have put him on his knees if he wasn't already sitting down. Still might. It didn't make any sense for her to be so unselfish with her time, her body, her cupcakes even without some gain other than the righteous promise of *friendship*. "I don't believe that's the whole reason."

A tiny frown marred her gorgeous mouth and he wished he could kiss it away. But he didn't move. This was something he should have questioned before they got on the plane.

"Is this another conversation about how you don't trust me?" she asked in a small voice.

Deserved that. He shook his head. "This is not a trust issue. It's that I don't understand what you're getting out of all of this. I've always wondered. I promised you that I would help you with your business since you claimed that as your passion. Then you politely declined all the success my efforts have produced. I give you the option to leave and you don't take it. Friendship doesn't seem like enough of a motivator."

Guilt crowded through her gaze. What was that all about? But she looked away before he got confirmation that it was indeed guilt, and he had a burning need to understand all at once.

The vows he'd taken with Warren and Hendrix after Marcus's death seemed like a pinky swear on the playground in comparison to Viv's friendship standards, yet he'd based his adult life on that vow. If there was something to learn from her about the bonds of friendship, he'd be an instant student.

Hooking her chin with his finger, he guided her face back toward his, feathering a thumb across her cheek before he'd barely gotten purchase. God, she felt so good. It was all he could do to keep from spreading his entire palm across her cheek, lifting her lips into a kiss that would resolve nothing other than the constant ache under his skin.

He'd enjoy every minute of the forbidden, though.

Since she still hadn't answered, he prompted her. "What's your real reason, Viv? Tell me why you'd do this for me after all I've said and done."

She blinked. "I agreed to this deal. You of all people should know that keeping your word is a choice. Anyone can break a promise but mine to you means something."

That wasn't it, or rather it wasn't the full extent. He could tell. While he appreciated her conviction, she was hedging. He hadn't expanded Kim Electronics into the American market and grown profits into the ten-figure range by missing signs that the person on the other side of the table wasn't being entirely forthcoming. But she wasn't a factory owner looking to make an extra million or two or a parts distributor with shady sources.

She was his wife. Why couldn't he take what she said at face value and leave it at that?

Because she hadn't told him about wanting a real marriage, that was why. It stuck under his rib cage, begging him to do something with that knowledge, and the answer wasn't pulling her into his arms like he wanted to. He should be cutting her free by his choice, not hers.

Yet Viv was quietly showing him how to be a real

friend regardless of the cost. It was humbling, and as the limo snaked through the crowded streets of Seoul toward his grandfather's house, his chest got so tight and full of that constant ache he got whenever he looked at Viv that he could hardly breathe.

Caught in the trap of his own making, he let his hand drop away from her face. He had a wife he couldn't let himself love and two friends he couldn't let himself disappoint. At what point did Jonas get what he wanted? And when had his desire for something more shifted so far away from what he had?

There was no good answer to that. The limo paused by his grandfather's gates as they opened and then the driver pulled onto the hushed property draped with trees and beautiful gardens. The ancestral home that Grandfather had given Jonas and Viv lay a kilometer down the road up on a hill. Both properties were palatial, befitting a businessman who entertained people from all over the world, as Jung-Su did. As Jonas would be expected to do when he stepped into Grandfather's shoes. He'd need a wife to help navigate the social aspects of being the CEO of a global company.

But the painful truth was that he couldn't imagine anyone other than Viv by his side. He needed *her*, not a wife, and for far more reasons than because it might or might not secure the promotion he'd been working toward. At the same time, as much as he'd denied that his questions were about trust, he was caught in a horrible catch-22. Trust *was* at the root of it.

Also a trap of his own making. He was predisposed to believe that a woman would string him along until she got tired of him and then she'd break his heart. So he looked for signs of that and pounced the moment he found evidence, when in reality, he'd have to actually give his heart to a woman before it could be broken. And that was what he was struggling to avoid.

Grandfather's *jibsa* ushered them into the house and showed them to their rooms. A different member of the staff discreetly saw to their needs and eventually guided Jonas and Viv to where his grandfather sat in the garden outside, enjoying the sunshine. The garden had been started by Jonas's grandmother, lovingly overseen until her death several years ago. Her essence still flitted among the mugunghwa blooms and bellflowers, and he liked remembering her out here.

His grandfather looked well, considering he'd recently been diagnosed with some precursors to heart disease and had begun rounds of medication to reverse the potential for a heart attack.

"Jonas. Miss Viviana." Grandfather smiled at them each in turn and Viv bent to kiss his cheek, which made the old man positively beam. "I'm pleased to see you looking well after your flight. It is not an easy one."

Viv waved that off and took a seat next to Jung-Su on the long stone bench. His grandfather sat on a cushion that was easier on his bones but Viv didn't seem to notice that she was seated directly on the cold rock ledge. Discreetly, Jonas flicked his fingers at one of the many uniformed servants in his grandfather's employ, and true to form, the man returned quickly with another cushion for her.

She took it with a smile and resituated herself, still chatting with Grandfather about the flight and her impressions of Korea thus far. Grandfather's gaze never left her face and Jonas didn't blame him. She was mesmerizing. Surrounded by the lush tropical beauty of the garden and animated by a subject that clearly intrigued her, she was downright breathtaking. Of course, Jonas was biased. Especially since he hadn't been able to take a deep breath pretty much since the moment he'd said *I do* to this woman.

"Jonas. Don't hover." Grandfather's brows came together as he shot a scowl over the head of his new granddaughter-in-law. "Sit with us. Your lovely wife was just telling me about baking cupcakes on the American television show."

"Yes, she was brilliant," Jonas acknowledged. But he didn't sit on the bench. The only open spot was next to Viv and it was entirely too much temptation for his starving body to be that near her.

"Jonas is too kind." Viv's nose wrinkled as she shook her head. "The show hasn't even aired yet."

"So? I don't have to see it to know that you killed it." Plus, she'd told him she'd won, like it was no big deal, when in fact, it was. Though the result was hardly shocking. "*Brilliant* is an understatement."

Viv ducked her head but not before he caught the pleased gleam in her eye. He should have told her that already and more than once. Instead, he'd been caught up in his own misery. She deserved to hear how wonderful she was on a continual basis.

"It's true," he continued. "She does something special with her recipes. No one else can touch her talent when it comes to baking."

Grandfather watched them both, his gaze traveling back and forth between them as if taking in a fascinating tennis match. "It's very telling that you are your wife's biggest fan."

Well, maybe so. But what it told, Jonas had no idea. He shrugged. "That's not a secret."

"It's a sign of maturity that I appreciate," his grandfather said. "For years I have watched you do nothing but work and I worried that you would never have a personal life. Now I see you are truly committed to your wife and I like seeing you happy. It only solidifies my decision to retire early."

Yeah. *Committed* described Jonas to a T. Committed to honor. Committed to making himself insane. Committed to the asylum might well be next, especially since his grandfather was so off the mark with his observation. But what was he supposed to do, correct him?

"It's only fair," Viv murmured before Jonas could formulate a response. "I'm his biggest fan, as well."

"Yes, I can see that, too," Jung-Su said with a laugh.

He could? Jonas glanced at Viv out of the corner of his eye in case there was some kind of sign emanating from her that he'd managed to miss. Except she had her sights firmly fixed on him and caught him eyeing her. Their gazes locked and he couldn't look away.

"You're a fan of workaholic, absentee husbands?" he asked with a wry smile of his own. Might as well own his faults in front of God and everyone.

"I'm a fan of your commitment, just like your grandfather said. You do everything with your heart. It's what I first noticed about you. You came into the shop to get cupcakes for your staff, and every time, I'd ask you 'What's the occasion today?' and you always knew the smallest details. 'It's Mrs. Nguyen's fiftieth birthday' or 'Today marks my admin's fourth anniversary working for me.' None of my other customers pay attention to stuff like that."

He shifted uncomfortably. Of course he knew those things. They'd been carefully researched excuses to buy cupcakes so he could see Viv without admitting he was there to see her. Granted, she'd already figured that out and blathered on about it to his parents during their first official married-couple dinner. Why bring that up again now?

"That's why he'll make the best CEO of Kim Global," she said to his grandfather as an aside. "Because he cares about people and cares about doing the right thing. He always keeps his word. His character is above reproach and honestly, that's why I fell for him."

That was laying it on a bit thick, but his grandfather just nodded. "Jonas is an honorable man. I'm pleased he's found a woman who loves him for the right reasons."

Except it was all fake. Jonas did a double take as Viv nodded, her eyes bright with something that looked a lot like unshed tears. "He's an easy man to love. My feelings for him have only grown now that we're married."

Jonas started to interrupt because…come on. There was playacting and there was outright lying to his grandfather for the sake of supporting Jonas's bid to become the next CEO. But as one tear slipped from her left eye, she glanced at him and whatever he'd been about to say vanished from his vocabulary. She wasn't lying.

He swallowed. Viv was in love with him? A band tightened around his lungs as he stared at her, soaking in the admission. It shouldn't be such a shock. She looked at him like that all the time. But not seconds after saying something so shocking, so provocative *out loud*. She couldn't take it back. It was out there, pinging around inside him like an arrow looking for a target.

A servant interrupted them, capturing Grandfather's attention, and everything fell apart as it became apparent that they were being called for dinner. Jonas took Viv's hand to help her to her feet as he'd done a hundred times before but her hand in his felt different, heavier somehow as if weighted with implications. She squeezed his hand as if she knew he needed her calming touch.

It was anything but calming. She was in love with him. The revelation bled through him. It was yet another thing that she'd held back from him that changed everything. He worked it over in his mind during dinner, longing to grab her and carry her out of this public room so he could ask her a few pointed questions. But Grandfather talked and talked and talked, and he'd invited a few business associates over as well, men Jonas couldn't ignore, given that the whole reason he was in Korea was to work through the transition as his grandfather stepped down.

Finally all the obstacles were out of the way and he cornered his wife in their room. She glanced up as he shut the door, leaning against it as he zeroed in on the woman sitting on the bed.

"That went well," she commented, her gaze cutting away from his. "Your grandfather seems like he's in good spirits after his diagnosis."

"I don't want to talk about that." He loved his grandfather, but they'd talked about his illness at length before Jonas had left the States, and he was satisfied he knew everything necessary about Jung-Su's health. Jonas's wife, on the other hand, needed to do a whole lot more talking and he needed a whole lot more understanding. "Why did you tell my grandfather that you're in love with me?"

"It just kind of…came out," she said. "But don't worry, I'm pretty sure he bought it."

"I bought it," he bit out. "It wasn't just something you said. You meant it. How long have you been in love with me?"

She shrugged. "It's not a big deal."

"It is a big deal!" Frustrated with the lack of headway, he crossed the room and stopped short of lifting her face so he could read for himself what she was feeling. But he didn't touch her, because he wanted her to own up to what was really going on inside. For once. "That's why you married me. Why you came to Korea. Why you're still here even though I told you about the pact."

That's when she met his gaze, steady and true. "Yes."

Something wonderful and beautiful and strong burst through his heart. It all made a lot more sense now. What he'd been calling friendship was something else entirely.

Now would be a *really* good time to sit down. So he did. "Why didn't you tell me? That's information that I should have had a long time ago."

"No, Jonas, it's not." She jammed her hands on her hips. "What does it change? Nothing. You're determined to keep your vow to your friends and I can't stop being in love with you. So we're both stuck."

Yes. *Stuck.* He'd been between a rock and a hard

place for an eternity because he couldn't stop being in love with her either.

He'd tried. He'd pretended that he wasn't, called it friendship, pushed her away, stayed away himself, thrown his honor down between them. But none of it had worked because he'd been falling for her since the first cupcake.

Maybe it was time to try something else.

"Viv." He stood and waited until he had her full attention. But then when she locked gazes with him, her expressive eyes held a world of possibilities. Not pain. Not destruction. None of the things that he'd tried to guard against.

That was the reason she should leave. Instead of feeling stuck, she should divorce him simply because he was a moron. The character she'd spoken of to his grandfather didn't include being courageous. He was a coward, refusing to acknowledge that avoiding love hadn't saved him any heartache. In fact, it had caused him a lot more than he'd credited. Had caused Viv a lot, too.

Worse, he'd avoided the wonderful parts, and ensured that he'd be lonely to boot. And what had he robbed himself of thus far? Lots of sex with his wife, a chance to have a real marriage and many, many moments where she looked at him like she was looking at him right now. As if he really was worthy of her devotion, despite his stupidity.

He'd had plenty of pain already. Avoiding the

truth hadn't stopped that. The lesson here? No more pretending.

"Tell me," he commanded. "No more hiding how you really feel. I want to hear it from you, no holds barred."

"Why are you doing this?" Another tear slipped down her face and she brushed it away before he could, which seemed to be a common theme. She had things inside that she didn't trust him with and he didn't blame her.

"Because we haven't been honest with each other. In fact, I'd say my behavior thus far in our marriage hasn't been anything close to honorable, and it's time to end that. You know what? I should go first then." He captured her hand and held it between his. "Viv. You're my friend, my lover, my wife, my everything. When I made a vow to never fall in love, it was from a place of ignorance. Because I thought love was a bad thing. Something to be avoided. You taught me differently. And I ignored the fact that I took vows with you. Vows that totally overshadow the promise I made to Warren and Hendrix before I fully understood what I was agreeing to give up. I'm not okay with that anymore. Not okay with pretending. What I'm trying to say, and not doing a very good job at, is that I love you, too."

Like magic, all of his fear vanished simply by virtue of saying it out loud. At last, he could breathe. The clearest sense of happiness radiated from somewhere deep inside and he truly couldn't fathom why it had taken him so long to get to this place.

Viv eyed him suspiciously instead of falling into his waiting arms. "What?"

He laughed but it didn't change her expression. "I love you. I wouldn't blame you if you needed to hear it a hundred more times to believe me."

Her lips quirked. "I was actually questioning the part where you said you weren't doing a good job explaining. Because it seemed pretty adequate to me."

That seemed like as good an invitation as any to sweep her into his arms. In a tangle, they fell back against the mattress, and before he could blink, she was kissing him, her mouth shaping his with demanding little pulls, as if she wanted everything inside him. He didn't mind. It all belonged to her anyway.

Just as he finally got his hands under her dress, nearly groaning at the hot expanse of skin that he couldn't wait to taste, she broke the kiss and rolled him under her.

That totally worked for him. But she didn't dive back in like his body screamed for her to. Instead, she let him drown in her warm brown eyes as she smiled. "What's going to happen when we get home and you have to explain to Warren and Hendrix that you broke your word to them?"

"Nothing. Because that's not what I'm going to say." He smoothed back a lock of her hair that had fallen into her face, and shifted until her body fell into the grooves of his perfectly. This position was his new favorite. "We made that pact because we didn't want to lose each other. Our friendship isn't threatened because I finally figured out that I'm in love with you. I'll help them realize that."

"Good. I don't want to be the woman who came between you and your friends."

"You couldn't possibly. Because you're the woman who *is* my friend. I never want that to change."

And then there was no more talking as Viv made short work of getting them both undressed, which was only fair since she was on top. He liked Take Charge Viv almost as much as he liked In Love with Him Viv.

She was everything he never expected when he fell in love with his best friend.

Epilogue

Jonas walked into the bar where he'd asked Warren and Hendrix to meet him. He'd tried to get Viv to come with him, but she'd declined with a laugh, arguing that the last person who should be present at the discussion of how Jonas had broken the pact was the woman he'd fallen in love with.

While he agreed, he still wasn't looking forward to it. Despite what he'd told Viv, he didn't think Warren and Hendrix were going to take his admission lightly.

His friends were already seated in a high-backed booth, which Jonas appreciated given the private nature of what he intended to discuss. They'd already taken the liberty of ordering, and three beers sat on the table. But when he slid into the booth across from Warren, Hendrix cleared his throat.

"I'm glad you called," Hendrix threw out before Jonas could open his mouth. "I have something really important to ask you both."

Thrilled to have an out, Jonas folded his hands and toyed with his wedding band, which he did anytime he thought about Viv. He did it so often, the metal had worn a raw place on his finger. "I'm all ears, man."

Warren set his phone down, but no less than five notifications blinked from the screen. "Talk fast. I have a crisis at work."

Hendrix rolled his eyes. "You always have a crisis. It's usually that you're not there. Whatever it is can wait five minutes." He let out a breath with a very un-Hendrix-like moan. "I need you guys to do me a favor and I need you to promise not to give me any grief over it."

"That's pretty much a guarantee that we will," Warren advised him with cocked eyebrow. "So spill before I drag it out of you."

"I'm getting married."

Jonas nearly spit out the beer he'd just sipped. "To one woman?"

"Yes, to one woman." Hendrix shot him a withering glare. "It's not that shocking."

"The hell you say." Warren hit the side of his head with the flat of his palm. Twice. "I think my brain is scrambled. Because I'd swear you just said you were getting married."

"I did, jerkoff." Hendrix shifted his scowl to Warren. "It's going to be very good for me."

"Did you steal that speech from your mom?" Warren jeered, his phone completely forgotten in favor of the real-life drama happening in their booth. "Because it sounds like you're talking about eating your veggies, not holy matrimony."

"You didn't give Jonas this much crap when he got married," Hendrix reminded him as Warren grinned.

"Um, whatever." Jonas held up a finger as he zeroed in on the small downturn of Hendrix's mouth. "That is completely false, first of all. You have a short memory. And second, if this is like my marriage, you're doing it for a reason, one you're not entirely happy about. What's this really about?"

Hendrix shrugged, wiping his expression clear. "I'm marrying Rosalind Carpenter. That should pretty much answer all of your questions."

It *so* did not. Warren and Jonas stared at him, but Warren beat him to the punch. "Whoa, dude. That's epic. Is she as much a knockout in person as she is in all those men's magazines?"

He got an elbow in his ribs for his trouble, but it wasn't Warren's fault that there were so many sexy pictures of Rosalind Carpenter to consider.

"Shut up. That's my fiancée you're talking about."

Jonas pounded on the table to get their attention. "On that note…if the question is will we be in the wedding party, of course we will." They had plenty of time to get the full story. After Jonas steered them back to the reason why he'd called them with an invitation for drinks. "Get back to us when you've made plans. Now chill out while we talk about my thing."

"Which is?" Warren gave him the side-eye while checking his messages.

"I broke the pact."

The phone slipped out of Warren's hand and thunked against the leather seat. "You did what? With Viv?"

Jonas nodded and kept his mouth shut as his friends lambasted him with their best shots at his character, the depths of his betrayal and the shallowness of his definition of the word *vow*. He took it all with grace because he didn't blame them for their anger. They just needed to experience the wonders of the right woman for themselves and then they'd get it.

When they were mostly done maligning him, Jonas put his palms flat on the table and leaned forward. "No one is more surprised by this than me. But it's the truth. I love her and I broke the pact. But it's not like it was with Marcus. She loves me back and we're happy. I hope you can be happy for us, too. Because we're going to be married and in love for a long time."

At least that was his plan. And by some miracle, it was Viv's, too.

"I can't believe you're doing this to us," Warren

shot back as if he hadn't heard a word Jonas said. "Does keeping your word mean nothing to you?"

"Integrity is important to me," he told them without blinking. "That's why I'm telling you the truth. Lying about it would dishonor my relationship with Viv. And I can't stop loving her just to stick to a pact we made. I tried and it made us both miserable."

"Seems appropriate for a guy who turns on his buddies," Hendrix grumbled.

"Yeah, we'll see how you feel after you get married," Jonas told him mildly. Hendrix would come around. They both would eventually. They'd been friends for too long to let something like a lifetime of happiness come between them, strictly over principle.

Warren griped about the pact for another solid five minutes and then blew out a breath. "I've said my piece and now I have to go deal with a distribution nightmare. This is not over."

With that ominous threat, Warren shoved out of the booth and stormed from the restaurant.

Hendrix, on the other hand, just grinned. "I know you didn't mean to break the pact. It's cool. Things happen. Thank God that'll never be me, but I'm happy that you're happy."

"Thanks, man." They shook on it and drank to a decade of friendship.

When Jonas got home, Viv was waiting in the foyer. His favorite. He flashed her the thumbs-up so she would know everything was okay between him and his friends—which it would be once Warren calmed down—then wrapped Viv in his arms and let her warmth infuse him. "I have another favor to ask."

"Anything."

No hesitation. That might be his favorite quality of hers. She was all in no matter what he asked of her—because she loved him. How had he gotten so lucky? "You're not even going to ask what it is?"

She shrugged. "If it's anything like the last favor, which landed me the hottest husband on the planet, by the way, why would I say no? Your favors are really a huge win for me so…"

Laughing, he kissed her and that made her giggle, too. His heart was so full, he worried for a moment that it might burst. "Well, I'm not sure this qualifies as a win. I was just going to ask you to never stop loving me."

"Oh, you're right. I get nothing out of that," she teased. "It's torture. You make me happier than I would have ever dreamed. Guess I can find a way to put up with that for the rest of my life."

"Good answer," he murmured, and kissed his wife, his lover, his friend. His everything.

* * * * *

If you loved this story,
pick up these other sexy and emotional reads
from USA TODAY bestselling author
Kat Cantrell!

TRIPLETS UNDER THE TREE
A PREGNANCY SCANDAL
THE PREGNANCY PROJECT
FROM ENEMIES TO EXPECTING
THE MARRIAGE CONTRACT

Available now from Harlequin Desire!

* * *

If you're on Twitter, tell us what you think of
Harlequin Desire! #harlequindesire

Read on for a sneak peek of
DOWN HOME COWBOY
by New York Times *bestselling author*
Maisey Yates.
When rancher and single dad Cain Donnelly
moves to Copper Ridge, Oregon, to make a fresh
start with his teenage daughter, the last thing
he wants is to risk his heart again. So why can't he
keep his eyes—or his hands—off Alison Davis,
the one woman in town guaranteed to
complicate his life?

"HEY, BO," CAIN CALLED, looking around the kitchen and living room area for his daughter, who was on the verge of being late for her second week on the job. "Are you ready to go?"

He heard footsteps hit the bottom landing, followed by a disgusted noise. "Do you have to call me that?"

"Yes," he said, keeping his tone serious. "Though I could always go back to the full name. Violet Beauregarde the Walking Blueberry." She'd thought that nod to *Charlie and the Chocolate Factory* was great. Back when she was four and all he'd had to do was smile funny to get her to belly laugh.

"Pass."

"I have to call you at least one horrifying nickname a week. All the better if it slips out in public."

"Is there public in Copper Ridge? Because I've yet to see it."

"Hey, you serve the public as part of your job at the bakery."

"The presence of humanity does not mean the presence of culture."

"Chill out, Sylvia Plath. Your commitment to being angry at the world is getting old." He shook his head, looking at his dark-haired, green-eyed daughter, who was now edging closer to being a woman than being that round, rosy-cheeked little girl he still saw in his mind's eye.

"Well, you don't have to bear witness to it today. Lane is giving me a ride into town."

Cain frowned. He still hadn't been in to see Violet at work. In part because she clearly didn't want him to. But he had assumed that once she was established and feeling independent she wouldn't mind if he took her to Pie in the Sky.

Apparently, she did.

"Great," he said. "I have more work to do around here anyway."

"The life of a dairy farmer is never dull. Well, no, it's always dull. It just never stops." Violet walked over to the couch where she had deposited her purse yesterday and picked it up. "Same with baking pies, I guess."

"Are you ready to go, Violet?" Lane came breezing into the room looking slightly disheveled, Cain's younger brother Finn closely behind her, also looking suspiciously mussed.

Absolutely no points for guessing what they had just been up to. Though he could see that Violet was oblivious. If she had guessed, she wouldn't be able to hide her reaction. Which warmed his heart in a way. That his teenage daughter was still pretty innocent about some things. That she was still young in some ways.

Hard to retain any sort of innocence when your mother abandoned you. And since he knew all about parental abandonment and how much it screwed with you, he was even angrier that his daughter was going through the same thing.

"Ready," Violet responded.

Even though it was a one-word answer, it lacked the edge usually involved in her responses to him. He supposed being jealous of his brother's girlfriend was a little bit ridiculous.

"Have fun," he said, just because he knew it would irritate her.

He had lost the power to make her laugh. To make her smile, with any kind of ease. So, he supposed he would just embrace his ability to irritate.

At least he excelled at that.

He could tell he had excelled yet again when she didn't smile at him as she left the room with Lane.

"Wait," Finn said, walking past him and grabbing Lane around the waist, turning her and kissing her deep.

It was all Cain could do to keep from groaning audibly. Between his horndog younger brothers and his incredibly happy other brother, he felt like sex was being thrown in his face constantly. Except not in a fun way that involved him having it.

Lane and Violet left, and Finn walked back into the living room. "I'm going to marry that woman," he said, the self-satisfied grin on his face scraping at Cain's current irritation.

"Have you asked her yet?"

"Not officially. But I'm going to. I want to spend the rest of my life with her."

"That's a long time. Trust me. Married years are different than regular years." He had way too much experience living with somebody who didn't even like him anymore. Way too much experience walking quietly through his own house so that he could avoid the conversation that needed to be had, or avoid the silence that seemed magnified when the two of them were in the same room.

He didn't think Finn would suffer the same fate, though. Finn and Lane had known each other for years, and they had been friends before they were a couple. Cain and Kathleen had been stupid and young. He had gotten her pregnant and wanted to do the right thing, instead of doing the kind of thing his father would do.

All in all, it wasn't the best foundation for a marriage.

For a while, they had tried. Both of them. He wasn't really sure when they had stopped.

"I hope you're right," Finn said, obnoxiously cheerful. "I hope every year with Lane feels like five. Because my time with her has been the best of my life."

Given the way they had grown up, Cain really didn't begrudge Finn his happiness. He was glad for his brother, in a way. When he wasn't busy feeling irritated by his own celibate status.

Though, in fairness to him, figuring out how to conduct a physical relationship while he was raising a teenage girl was pretty tricky. He had to set some kind of example. And casual sex wasn't exactly the one he was aiming for.

"Good for you," he said, sounding more annoyed than he had intended.

"How's the barn coming along?"

Cain was grateful for the change in subject. "It's coming."

"Show me."

His brother grabbed his hat off the shelf by the door, and Cain grabbed his own. Strange how this had become somewhat natural. How sharing a space with Finn, Alex and Liam—while annoying on occasion—was just starting to be life.

He took the steps on the front porch two at a time, inhaling the sharp, clear air. It was late summer, and in Texas about now walking outside would be like getting wrapped in a wet blanket. That was also on fire. He could honestly say he didn't miss that part of his adopted home state.

The Oregon coast ran a little cold for his taste, but he had to admit it was still nicer than sweltering. The wind whipped up, filtering through the pine trees and kicking up the smell of wood, hay and horse. If green had a smell, it would be that smell that rode the coastal air across the mountains. Fresh and heavy, all at the same time.

It was fastest to take a truck out to the old barn on the property, the one that had originally stood near the first house that had been built when their great-grandparents had bought the land. The house was long gone, but the barn still remained, and with all of his near-nonexistent free time, Cain had been fashioning the place into a house for Violet and himself.

After they parked, he and his brother walked through the still overgrown pathway that led up to the old barn.

"Wow," Finn said, stepping deeper into the room. "You've done a lot."

"New wiring," Cain said, gesturing broadly. "Insulation, Sheetrock. I need to work on interior walls. But, yeah, it's coming along. It will be fine for the two of us for the next couple of years. And when Violet leaves…"

Unbidden, an image of the beautiful redhead he had seen across the bar last night filtered into his mind's eye. Yeah, in a couple of years he would have a place to bring a woman like that.

Not that he couldn't go back to her place, or get a hotel, but he didn't want to have to explain his absence to a teenage girl who barely thought of him as human, much less wanted to realize he was actually just a guy with a sex drive and everything. Both of them would probably die from the humiliation of that.

"It'll be a pretty nice place," Finn said, and Cain was grateful his younger brother couldn't read his mind.

"Not bad. I know that I could pay somebody to finish it. But right now I'm kind of enjoying the therapy. I spent a long time managing things. Managing a big ranch, not actually working it. Managing my marriage instead of actually working at it. I'm ready to be hands-on again. This is the life that I'm choosing to build for myself. So I guess I better build it."

He knew that at thirty-eight his feelings of midlife angst were totally unearned, but having his wife leave had forced him into kind of a strange crisis point. One where he had started asking himself if that was it. If everything good that he was going to do was behind him.

So, he had left the ranch in Texas—the one he had spent so many years building up—walked away with a decent chunk of change, and packed his entire life up, packed his kid up, and gone to the West Coast to find… Something else to do. Something else to be. To find a way to reconnect with Violet.

So far, he'd found ranch work and little else. Violet still barely tolerated him in spite of everything he was doing to try to fix their lives, and he didn't feel any closer to moving forward than he had back in Texas.

He was just moved.

Finn's phone buzzed and he pulled it out of his

pocket to check his texts. "Hey," he said, "can you pick up Violet tonight from work?"

"I thought Lane was doing it."

"It's her girls' night thing. She forgot."

Well, he had just been thinking that he needed to actually see where Violet worked. "Sure. Sounds good."

"What are you going to do until then?"

"I figured I would do some work in here."

Finn pushed his sleeves up, smiling. "Mind if I help?"

"Sure," Cain said. "Grab a hammer."

ALISON STARED AT the sunken cake sitting on the kitchen countertop and frowned. Then quickly erased the frown so that Violet wouldn't see it.

"I don't know what happened," Violet said, looking perturbed.

"You probably took it out too early. It's nothing a little extra icing can't fix. And it's my girls' night tonight, so I think it can be of use in that environment rather than being put up for sale."

Violet screwed up her face. "It's ugly."

"An ugly cake is still cake. As long as it doesn't have raisins it's fine."

"Oh, I didn't put any raisins in it."

Alison was slightly amused that her newest employee seemed to know about her raisin aversion, even if she didn't quite have cooking times down. Violet was a good employee, but she had absolutely no experience baking. For the most part, Alison had put her on the register, which she had picked up much faster than kitchen duties. But she tried to set aside a certain amount of time every shift to give Violet a chance to get some experience with the actual baking part of the bakery.

Maybe it wasn't as necessary to do with a teenager who had her first job as it was to do with some of the other women who came through the shop, desperately in need of work experience after years out of the workforce, but Alison was applying the same principles to Violet as she did to everyone else.

Right now she was short on staff, and even shorter on people who had the skill level she required with the baked goods to do any training. So while she could farm out Violet's register training, the cakes, pies and other pastries had to be done by her.

"I'll do better next time," Violet said, sounding determined. Which encouraged Alison, because Violet hadn't sounded anything like determined when she had first come in looking for work. Violet was a sullen teenager of the first order. And even though she most definitely made an attempt to put on a good show for Alison, she was clearly in a full internal battle with her feelings on authority figures.

Having been a horrific teenager herself, Alison felt some level of sympathy for her. But also very little patience. Fortunately, Violet seemed to react well to her brand of no-nonsense response to attitude.

"You will do better next time," Alison said, "because I can eat one mistake cake, but if I have to continue eating them, my jeans aren't going to fit and then I'm going to have to buy new jeans, and that's going to have to come out of your paycheck."

She patted Violet on the shoulder then walked through the double doors that led from the kitchen and behind the counter. The shop was in its late-afternoon lull. A little too close to dinner for most people to be stopping in for pieces of pie.

A rush of air blew into the shop and Alison looked up just in time to see a tall, muscular man walk in through the blue door. A pang of recognition hit her in the chest before she even got a good look at him. She didn't need a good look at him. Because just like the first time she'd seen him, on the other side of Ace's bar, the feeling he created inside of her wasn't logical, wasn't cerebral. It was physical. It lived in her, and it superseded control.

For somebody who prized control, it was an affront on multiple levels.

He lifted his head and confirmed what her jittering nerves already knew. That beneath that dark cowboy hat was the face of the man who had most definitely been looking at her at the bar the night before.

He hadn't left town. He hadn't been a hallucinogenic expression of a fevered imagination. And he had found her.

The twist of attraction turned into something else, just for a moment. A strange kind of panic that she hadn't confronted for a long time. That somehow this man had found out who she was, had tracked her down.

No. That's not it. Even if he did, that doesn't make him crazy. It doesn't.

And more than likely he was just here for a piece of pie. She took a deep breath, steeling herself to look directly at him. Which was... Wow. He was hotter than she remembered. And that was saying something. She had first spotted him in the dim light of the bar, with a healthy amount of space between them.

Now, well, now the daylight was bright, and he was very close. And he was magnificent. The way that black T-shirt hugged all those muscles bordered on obscene, his dark green eyes like the deep of the forest beckoning her to draw close. Except, unlike the forest, his eyes didn't promise solitude and inner peace. No, it was something much more carnal. Or maybe that was just her aforementioned overheated imagination.

His jaw was covered by a neatly trimmed dark beard, and she would normally have said she wasn't a huge fan, but something about the beard on him was like flaunting an excess of testosterone. And she was in a very testosterone-starved state. So it was like stumbling onto water in a desert.

Of course, all of that hyperbole was simply that. His eyes weren't actually promising her anything; in fact, his expression was blank. And she realized that while he might look sexier to her today than he had that night, she might look unrecognizable to him.

Last night she had been wearing an outfit that at least hinted at the fact that she had a female figure. And she'd had makeup on. Plus, she'd gone to the effort to straighten her mass of auburn hair. Today, it was its glorious frizzy self, piled on top of her head, half captured in a rubber band, half pinned down with a pen. And as for makeup… Well, on days when she had to be at the bakery early, that was just not a happening thing.

Her apron disguised her figure, and beneath it, the button-up striped shirt that she had tucked into her jeans wasn't exactly vixen wear.

"Can I…? Can I help you?" She tucked a stray strand of hair behind her ear and found herself tilting her head to the side, her body apparently calling on all of the flirtation skills it hadn't used since she was eighteen years old.

Very immature, underdeveloped skills.

Suddenly, her lips felt dry, so she had to lick them. And when she did, heat flared in those forest green eyes that made her think maybe he did recognize her. Or, if he didn't, maybe his body did. Just like hers recognized his. *Oh, Lord.*

"Yes," he said, his voice much more…taciturn than she had imagined it might be. She hadn't realized until that moment that she had built something of a narrative around him. Brooding, certainly, because he had most definitely been brooding in the bar, but she had imagined he might flirt with a lazy drawl. Of course, it was difficult to tell with one word, but his voice had been clipped. Definitely clipped.

"I have a lot of different pie. I mean, a lot of different kinds. So, if you need suggestions…or a list… I can help."

"I'm not here for pie. I'm here to pick up my daughter…"

Pick up DOWN HOME COWBOY,
the latest COPPER RIDGE *novel*
from Maisey Yates and HQN Books!

Get 2 Free Books,
Plus 2 Free Gifts—
just for trying the Reader Service!

HARLEQUIN *Desire*

YES! Please send me 2 FREE Harlequin® Desire novels and my 2 FREE gifts (gifts are worth about $10 retail). After receiving them, if I don't wish to receive any more books, I can return the shipping statement marked "cancel." If I don't cancel, I will receive 6 brand-new novels every month and be billed just $4.80 per book in the U.S. or $5.49 per book in Canada. That's a savings of at least 8% off the cover price! It's quite a bargain! Shipping and handling is just 50¢ per book in the U.S. and 75¢ per book in Canada.* I understand that accepting the 2 free books and gifts places me under no obligation to buy anything. I can always return a shipment and cancel at any time. The free books and gifts are mine to keep no matter what I decide.

225/326 HDN GLWG

Name _____ (PLEASE PRINT) _____

Address _____ Apt. #

City _____ State/Prov. _____ Zip/Postal Code

Signature (if under 18, a parent or guardian must sign)

Mail to the **Reader Service:**
IN U.S.A.: P.O. Box 1341, Buffalo, NY 14240-8531
IN CANADA: P.O. Box 603, Fort Erie, Ontario L2A 5X3

Want to try two free books from another line?
Call 1-800-873-8635 or visit www.ReaderService.com.

*Terms and prices subject to change without notice. Prices do not include applicable taxes. Sales tax applicable in N.Y. Canadian residents will be charged applicable taxes. Offer not valid in Quebec. This offer is limited to one order per household. Books received may not be as shown. Not valid for current subscribers to Harlequin Desire books. All orders subject to approval. Credit or debit balances in a customer's account(s) may be offset by any other outstanding balance owed by or to the customer. Please allow 4 to 6 weeks for delivery. Offer available while quantities last.

Your Privacy—The Reader Service is committed to protecting your privacy. Our Privacy Policy is available online at www.ReaderService.com or upon request from the Reader Service.

We make a portion of our mailing list available to reputable third parties that offer products we believe may interest you. If you prefer that we not exchange your name with third parties, or if you wish to clarify or modify your communication preferences, please visit us at www.ReaderService.com/consumerschoice or write to us at Reader Service Preference Service, P.O. Box 9062, Buffalo, NY 14062-9062. Include your complete name and address.

HDI7R

SPECIAL EXCERPT FROM

H HARLEQUIN

Desire

*When billionaire Linc Ballantyne's ex abandons not
one, but two children, he strikes up a wary deal with her
too-sexy sister. She'll be the nanny and they'll keep their
hands to themselves. But their temporary truce soon
becomes a temporary tryst!*

*Read on for a sneak peek at
THE CEO'S NANNY AFFAIR
by Joss Wood.*

Why Linc had ever agreed to meet with his ex-fiancée's
sister was confounding. But he'd heard something in her
voice, a note of panic and sorrow. Maybe something had
happened to Kari, and, if so, he needed to know what.
She was still his son's mother, after all.

Linc heard the light rap on the door and sucked in a
breath.

His first thought when he opened his front door to Tate
Harper was that he wanted her. Under him, on top of him,
up against the nearest wall…any way he could have her.

That thought was immediately followed by *Oh, crap,
not again.*

He knew the Harpers were trouble. Kari had been a
stunning woman, but her beauty, as he knew—and paid
for—had taken work. The woman standing behind the
stroller was effortlessly gorgeous. Her hair was a riot of

blond and brown, eyes the color of his favorite whiskey under arched eyebrows, and her skin, makeup-free, was flawless. This Harper sister's beauty was all natural and, dammit, so much more potent.

Linc, his hand on the doorknob, took a moment to draw in some much-needed air.

"Tate? Come on in."

She pushed the stroller into the hall with a white-knuckled grip. Linc, wincing at the realization that he was allowing a whole bunch of trouble to walk through his front door, was about to rescind his invitation. Then he made the mistake of looking into her eyes.

She'd jumped into the ring with Kari and had the crap kicked out of her, Linc realized. And, for some reason, she thought he could help her clean up the mess. And because his first instinct was to protect, to make things right, he wanted to wipe the fear from Tate's expression.

Linc closed his eyes and reminded himself to start using his brain.

He needed to hear Tate's story so he could hustle her out the door and get back to his predictable, safe, sensible world. She was pure temptation, and being attracted to his crazy ex's sister was a complication he most definitely did not need.

Don't miss
THE CEO'S NANNY AFFAIR
by Joss Wood, available August 2017 wherever
Harlequin® Desire books and ebooks are sold.

www.Harlequin.com

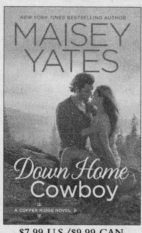

LOVE
Harlequin
romance?

Join our Harlequin community to share your thoughts and connect with other romance readers!

Be the first to find out about promotions, news, and exclusive content!

Sign up for the Harlequin e-newsletter and download a free book from any series at

www.TryHarlequin.com

CONNECT WITH US AT:

Harlequin.com/Community

 Facebook.com/HarlequinBooks

 Twitter.com/HarlequinBooks

 Instagram.com/HarlequinBooks

 Pinterest.com/HarlequinBooks

ReaderService.com

**ROMANCE WHEN
YOU NEED IT**

HSOCIAL2017

Want to give in to temptation with
steamy tales of irresistible desire?

Check out **Harlequin® Presents®**,
Harlequin® Desire and
Harlequin® Kimani™ Romance books!

New books available every month!

CONNECT WITH US AT:

Harlequin.com/Community

 Facebook.com/HarlequinBooks

 Twitter.com/HarlequinBooks

 Instagram.com/HarlequinBooks

 Pinterest.com/HarlequinBooks

ReaderService.com

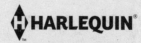

**ROMANCE WHEN
YOU NEED IT**